BEWARE THE LIGHT
AN ANTHOLOGY OF DARK FICTION

Naomi Artemi

Devin Hunt

Cheyenne Shaffer

Kyle Thompson

Keegan Young

**INK ALCHEMY
BOOKS**

Compilation copyright © 2024 by Ink Alchemy Books

Trade Paperback ISBN: 979-8-9906798-0-1
eBook ISBN: 979-8-9906798-1-8

Library of Congress Control Number: 2024909630

All rights reserved. Published in the United States
by Ink Alchemy Books, New York.

Cover Art by Nicholas Daniluk

inkalchemybooks.com

For my found one.
—NAOMI ARTEMI

To all the families in my life,
I write for you and because of you.
—DEVIN HUNT

To everyone who helped teach me to
think for myself and question what's
considered "normal."
—CHEYENNE SHAFFER

For Kim: Thanks for letting me talk so
much nonsense at you all these years.
I love you.
—KYLE THOMPSON

For my son, a greater gift than any gold.
—KEEGAN YOUNG

CONTENTS

THE DEVOUT

Cheyenne Shaffer

Part One

Rodrick
Truth or Consequences, New Mexico – May 5ᵗʰ, 2062

In the darkness of his cramped studio apartment on what would hopefully become the best night of his life, Roddy waited. The fridge hummed, his palms sweat, his ass fell asleep, and he waited. Still, he only got to review his plans for the evening twice in his head before she knocked. He could've used more time.

Standing, he tucked the folding chair beneath his desk and wiped shaking hands on his jeans. He turned the doorknob, and there she was. Jan. It was seven thirty, and the orange glow of twilight set her auburn curls on fire.

"Hey." He leaned over, planting a kiss on her freckled cheek.

She squinted into his apartment. "Were you sitting in the dark?"

"I have a surprise for you." He clapped, and a dozen strings of fairy lights flared to life above them. They hung from disposable mini-drones from the ten-dollar store, but that didn't diminish the effect. The drones spun in a pre-programmed pattern, turning the air above Roddy and Jan into a swirling vortex of light.

Jan clapped a hand to her mouth. "It's beautiful."

"There's more." He tapped a panel on the wall, and the opening chord of "Dance of the Angels," Jan's favorite tangopunk song, filtered through the apartment's speaker system. He reached for her hand and pulled her close.

She smiled, eyes uncertain. "What are you doing? You don't dance."

"But you do." As his hand found the curve of her back, his heart pounded as though he'd already finished dancing. "I might have done some research."

"Really?"

"Just the basics." He winked, the singer's voice belted out the first line, and they were off.

Almost immediately, his bare toes landed on the smooth edge of her boot. "Hey!" she said, laughing.

"There's a reason I wanted to do this while you still had shoes on." He smiled and spun them both around.

She kicked out a leg, dragging it sensuously in a circle around them. It took everything he had to keep the hand on her back from traveling downward.

"You're good," he said.

"You've seen me dance before."

"Not like this. I can appreciate it more when I'm trying to keep up."

"Want me to lead?"

He dipped her, drinking in the elegant curve of her neck. "And have to dance backward? No thank you."

"You're really not bad for a beginner." They stopped again, and she hiked her knee up against his hip. "Maybe I'll get brave and take my shoes off."

His hand strayed to her leg, holding it up. "It's very different to do this with another person." He stroked her thigh with his thumb. "Way more fun. No offense to the air I was practicing with earlier."

She rested her hand gently over his. "I'm sure it'll forgive you." With barely a rustle of fabric, she slipped her leg from his grasp, and they started moving again.

Pressure rose in his chest as the song built toward its conclusion. He needed to time this exactly right. Which beat did he start on again? In his concentration, his toes scuffed against the floor, and he stumbled.

She chuckled. "Sure it was a good idea to lead?"

"Yeah," he said, hearing the beat he'd always started with in practice. Perfect timing. "Otherwise, I couldn't do this."

He spun her away right as the music swelled into the final notes. Just as he knew she would, she ended the song with a dramatic pose, facing their imaginary audience. Instead of matching her, he dropped to one knee on the song's final beat, pulling a small box from his pocket.

"Jan," he said, squeezing her hand to draw her eyes toward him again, "will you marry me?"

He'd imagined so many different reactions—laughter; tears of joy; even a moment of quiet hesitation, as if she feared the proposal were some prank—but the sharp frown came as a surprise.

Her voice was small in the silence following the song. "Do you believe?"

Shit. "I've gone to church with you every week for months."

"Not what I asked."

He scanned the room as though he'd find a way out of the conversation tucked among the shifting shadows. Of course, there was none, and he refused to begin his marriage with a lie. "No. I don't believe. Does it really matter?"

She pulled her hand away, crossing her arms over her chest. "It's the law."

"It's a stupid law."

"My religion is stupid to you?"

"No, but mandating it is." He stood up, because fuck it. He wasn't going to argue with her while down on one knee.

"Until you, I never understood why it even had to be mandated. God's love is so beautiful. How could anyone not want it?"

He reached for her wrist, clutching it gently. "*Your* love is beautiful. I want that. I'd do anything for it."

She shook off his grasp. "Almost anything."

"You don't think I'd believe if I could? It's not some switch I can flip because it's convenient. I need evidence."

"But you'll go to Hell. Don't you understand?" Her voice broke. "I can't spend the rest of my life loving someone, knowing that's what awaits them. I'm not strong enough."

He snapped the ring box shut. "I'm sorry. I didn't realize it was such a burden, loving me."

"Don't."

He pushed the pain back, let it live beside him like pain always did. His feelings weren't worth losing Jan. "I won't mention it again if you don't. I'll go to church with you every week for the rest of my life. I'll be the perfect Christian. Whatever you want. I'll lie to the world. Just don't ask me to lie to you. Please."

She stood still a moment, not looking at him. Then it came—a quick, stifled sob—and he knew. With how many times they'd bared their emotions to one another in the past, she wouldn't try to hide this now if he hadn't already lost her.

"I'm sorry, Roddy," she said, her voice tight. "I can't live like that. I won't."

He swallowed. "And I'm sorry that's the only life I can give you."

She nodded, as though this confirmed something. "Then I guess I should be going." She took a deep breath, then added, "Don't worry. I'm not going to report you."

"Thanks," he said, though he hadn't been worried. Nothing that happened after this really mattered.

For a moment, they stared at one another, two years of love weighing down the air between them. Then, Jan turned and, without another word, walked out.

She never had taken off those shoes.

Roddy wasn't sure how long he stood there before he stopped staring at the door. Eventually, he just did, crossing the room to sink into the bed. An arm stretched mechanically toward the sleeping pills on his nightstand, and he curled up, cupping the bottle in one hand. How easy it would be to take one, as always, and drift into an unfeeling sleep. Perhaps in his dreams, they would still be together.

Perhaps in his dreams, he'd believe.

But he shook his head. Nothing about this night had been easy, and his dreams would be more of the same. Why face them?

He unscrewed the lid and let a wave of pills cascade into his palm.

Jules
New York City, New York – May 6ᵗʰ, 2062

As soon as her mom's phone rang, Jules knew she was in trouble. She heard it all the way from her room, 'cause Gen Alpha thought it was sooo cool for their phones to make noise the way those old corded phones in history books used to, and of course her mom was one-hundred percent AlphaHole.

A month ago, Jules wouldn't have thought twice about the sound. Her mom's phone had been going off six times a day, spouting the chorus of "Ur Fone"—which AlphaHoles thought was a hilariously ironic ringtone—every time some scammer rando-dialed her. But since she'd updated her SkamBlok, the apartment had been quiet. After all, phone calls were only for scammers or serious business. Now, hearing the thirty-year-old pop song blaring from the phone's tinny speakers, Jules could only think of one reason someone might have serious business with her mom.

She kept playing her video game, Cosmic Warfare II, as if acting innocent could change anything. Maybe some scammer had already found their way around the new update. But no. The floorboards creaked under her mother's weight as she stood. RIP

Jules in three . . . two . . . one.

"Jules." Her mother hammered on the door. "Open up. We need to talk."

For a moment, she tried to imagine an alternative to opening her door. Sneaking out the window? Kids did it all the time in those old-fashioned sitcoms about small-town America, but try it from a fifth floor walkup. She could throw on her headphones and pretend not to notice her mom, but that wouldn't last long, and her mom would just be twice as mad. She sighed. Sometimes in her game, the only option was to run toward the enemy, guns blazing. She pictured herself as the main character—Ava Shadow, all decked out in Kevlar and thick-soled boots—as she crossed the room to answer.

She opened the door. "What's up?" As if she didn't know.

Her mom crossed the threshold without waiting for an invitation. "Miss O'Brien called. Sounds like you said some interesting things in class today."

"Yeah?" The controller still hung from Jules' left hand, and she ran her thumb gently over the worn joystick.

"About aliens?"

Jules shrugged. "Aliens are interesting."

"They're fictional, Jules."

"And you would know? You've been to every planet?"

"We don't have to experience something to know it's true. God tells us so."

Jules flopped down onto her bed. "What part of the Bible is that again? Martians 3:16?"

"Don't be cute."

Jules hated when her mom said that. All her life, it was, *Oh, you're such a cute kid*—or, now that she was nearly thirteen, *I'm sure the boys all think you're cute*—but the second she said something her mom didn't like, suddenly it was, *Don't be cute.* Make up your mind.

"Why were you telling the other kids that aliens exist?" her mom asked.

"I read about it. Do you know how many people in history have claimed to see them?"

"*Claimed*, honey. People claim all kinds of things. The Church has looked into all that, and you know they've discredited it. Their official stance is that all God's living creatures are right here on Earth."

"And you just believe them?"

"They're the Church." Her mom laughed.

Jules didn't. She just dropped her gaze back to the controller, rotating it in her hands.

"You believe what the Church tells us, don't you?" The humor had gone out of her mom's voice. Now, it carried a sharp edge.

"I don't know," Jules mumbled.

"You don't know?"

She sat up, her voice gaining strength. "No, I guess I don't."

"Why not?"

"Because I don't get what makes them the experts on, like, everything. Johnny says they didn't even run the country until like 2030-something. He says before that, we specifically *didn't* have to be all Christians, and there were even different types of Christians. It was called 'freedom of religion.' Did you know that?"

"I know I might have to talk with Johnny's mother."

"But did you?"

"Of course I knew, honey. I was alive back then, before the Christian Unity. Just a kid, but still."

How old *was* her mom, anyway? "So if the Church knows everything, why weren't they always in charge?"

Her mom settled onto the bed beside her. "Nothing starts out perfect. You try things one way, and if they don't work, you change them to make them better. Over time, we realized letting the Church be in charge would be the best for everybody, so we did it."

"But if some people weren't Christians before, how was that the best for them?"

"Becoming Christian is the best thing for everybody. Don't you think?"

Jules laid the controller on the bed beside her; clearly, she wouldn't be getting back to her game anytime soon. "I guess I don't feel like it's that big a deal in my life."

She'd expected an explosion, but her mom was surprisingly calm as she asked, "Why is that?"

Jules paused, considering. "It doesn't feel real. I can pray, but it's not like getting God on the phone and hearing His voice. People say God talks to them, but that's not really what they mean, you know? And there are supposed to be angels and things. I can't imagine seeing something like that in real life. Can you?"

"No," her mom said, and Jules expected her to look surprised, as though these were all new ideas to her. She didn't. "But it's meant to be that way. If it were easy to prove, it wouldn't be faith."

Jules still didn't understand why faith would be more valuable than proof, but the first notes of 'Ur Fone' blasted from her mom's pocket, saving her from having to ask.

"Hello?" her mom said.

Jules couldn't remember doing anything else to earn a phone call home. Maybe this really was a scam.

A frown creased her mom's face. "No, why?"

Okay, definitely not a scammer. What could Jules possibly be in trouble for now?

"TV," her mom said, though still on the phone, "channel six."

The television flickered at her command, replacing Jules' game with footage of a desert town. A blue banner at the bottom of the screen read nonsensically, *Divine Judgment at Truth or Consequences?* In the video, flat-topped buildings lined the streets, some in surprisingly bright colors, but no one went in or out of any of them. Something was wrong. Cars weren't moving on the road; most were parked, though it looked like one or two had crashed or even been abandoned. A couple times, the panning camera offered a brief glimpse of what looked like piles of clothes on the sidewalk. It seemed absurd.

"—however, all attempts so far have been unsuccessful," a female newscaster's voice said over the footage. "Government officials are convening now to discuss the police's next course of action."

The video cut to a generic-looking older man in a suit. "This has been an absolute tragedy for New Mexico and the whole United States, and I won't rest until that beast is back in Hell, where it belongs."

The word *tragedy* stuck in Jules' head. Those hadn't been piles of clothes on the sidewalk. Those had been bodies.

By that point, her mom had excused herself from her phone conversation and was watching along. Tears ran down her cheeks, but she barely breathed.

"Mom, what is this?" Jules asked.

"It's your proof." She pointed at the screen. The video had changed again, this time showing something otherworldly. A dark shape with too many legs shifted in an alley, contrasting unsettlingly with the brightly colored buildings around it. It was huge, its head nearly level with the roof of the house it huddled against. "Hell has sent us a demon."

Rodrick
Truth or Consequences, New Mexico – May 7ᵗʰ, 2062

Roddy's consciousness took both a moment and an eternity to wade back to him through the black sludge in his mind. When it reached him, it didn't like what it found. His head pounded, his mouth tasted sour, and the acidic bite of vomit stung his nostrils. Still, he had the overwhelming feeling that something even worse lurked just beyond his comprehension.

He pried one eye open before slamming it shut again with a curse. So bright. Groaning, he shifted one aching arm up to block the light, then opened his eyes again. He was facing the wall, and the room around him seemed to glow. Slowly, his eyes adjusted, and when he was ready, he lifted his head.

Vomit crusted his pillow. Thank fuck he was a side sleeper. He hefted himself onto one arm, and as he moved, something caught at his ankles—a wire? He kicked it off, and his pill bottle rolled toward him across the mattress. With it came memories. The lights. The tango. Jan.

Maybe he should've been a back sleeper, after all.

Sitting up, he understood why the apartment was glowing: the fairy lights. The disposable drones had died, falling from the air while he slept, but the strands themselves, run on higher-quality battery packs, still glowed. They lit up his floor and furniture like a drunken airport runway.

He pulled his knees against his chest and threw the pill bottle, denting the drywall. A wail poured from his throat, followed by another.

In time, he quieted. His hands slipped from where he'd fisted them into his long, knotted hair. They came away greasy, and he wiped them on the bed. How long had he slept? A void opened in his stomach at the question. If hunger was any sign, he'd been out a while.

He stood, and his whole body ached. For a minute, he considered sliding back into bed and trying to forget he'd ever woken up, but the hunger wouldn't let him. He hobbled across the room to scrub at his lips with a wet paper towel, then he slipped on his shoes. If he was going to eat, he wanted to do it without reminders of last night glowing in his face.

He stepped outside. The sun warmed his skin, and a slight breeze played at his hair. He breathed deeply. One beautiful day wasn't enough of a reason to live, but since he hadn't died yet, he might as well appreciate it.

He started for the sidewalk, his head too sludgy to trust himself behind the wheel, and he followed Seventh until it reached the highway. Almost immediately, goosebumps climbed his arms. It was dead out here. He hadn't thought much about the quiet near his apartment, but the highway never went long without a car passing by. Not in the middle of the day. He stared down the flat road as far as his eyesight could carry him. An SUV was parked haphazardly on the roadside a ways away, looking abandoned. Otherwise, there was nothing.

No one was out in the parking lots, either, not even at the two motels across the street, which should have had maid service running at this point in the afternoon. Maybe he'd just come at a weird time. It was Sunday, after all—a mandated day of rest for non-essential workers, with worship accommodations for those who worked. Probably, the maids were on a prayer break. Any minute now, someone would step outside and break the spell. But no one did.

A garage sat ahead on the left: Flint's. Roddy hated walking past it. The sounds of whirring machinery, blaring rapcore, and occasional swearing always bled out to the sidewalk, feeling vaguely threatening, even with chain link fencing it in. Today, though, he missed the noise. The garage was silent, and a mixture of classic cars and rusted-out junkers sat haphazardly around the lot like someone had been in the middle of rearranging them and just got raptured.

Wait. Could this actually be the rapture? Jan had mentioned it a few times, but not in the way she talked about God or the Bible or the other things she really believed in. It seemed more like optional Christian lore, the kind of thing they'd invented to hold over the heads of sinners. Still, wouldn't that just figure; a lifelong heathen loses the only good thing in his life because he doesn't believe, then all the actual believers are taken to heaven, proving him wrong. At least if that was the case, he'd finally have his evidence. But would the world really be this quiet? Illegal or not, he couldn't be the only atheist in Truth or Consequences.

He reached the diner. Maybe when he stepped inside, the host would greet him with a smile and prove this was all just paranoia. He opened the door, and his stomach sank. The host's podium stood abandoned, though generic music still pumped through the speakers. He crept forward, peering into the dining room. Empty, but not untouched. Dirty dishes with half-eaten meals still lay at their places, and one of the tables was overturned. The smell of something foul yet sickly sweet tickled his nostrils, and a sense of dread told him to retreat back outside.

As he exited, something in the parking lot caught his eye—not movement, but a discoloration of the pavement. He approached, finding a dark red spot almost as big around as he was tall. He could only think of one thing that would turn the pavement that rusty color.

He backtracked to the garage and peered through the chain-link fence. The only red stains he could see from here were legit rust, but—wait. His eyes caught on a lumpy shape in the window of one of the cars. It was much too still and quiet to be a living thing, but it looked a hell of a lot like a person slumped in the driver's seat.

His heart pounded in his chest. This wasn't a rapture. Had the whole town been massacred? Jan flashed through his mind. Please, let her have gotten somewhere safe before this started.

His fingers stretched toward his phone as he entertained the notion of calling 911, but he stilled his hand. This wasn't just an average shooting. Who's to say the government itself wasn't behind this? If so, he wasn't about to light up their phones and tell them that hey, they missed one. Life was shit, but there were better ways to die than whatever this was.

Voices muttered. He froze when he heard them, honing in on the sound. Someone was alive out there—multiple someones. It occurred to him that they could have a bead on him, that he could be making their jobs all too easy by standing still, but why mutter before you pulled the trigger? No, they could've dropped him long ago if that was their aim.

The voices came from across the street, where an abandoned building stood, white with a western-style wooden storefront. Roddy crept toward it, feeling dumb for looking both ways as he scurried across the empty highway. When he reached the building, he pressed against the wall to listen. There were definitely voices inside, plural. Survivors or the ones who did the killing?

"We have it contained," someone said. "Now what? Do we really want to try moving this sucker?"

'It'? An 'it' had done this to everyone?

"Orders are to stay put." This second voice spoke in a way that expected no argument.

"We're gonna need fortifications if we're keeping it here long-term."

Roddy couldn't help himself. He peeked through the corner of a window. A few figures stood clustered against a door in full riot gear. No 'it's in sight.

"Hands in the air." That voice came from behind him.

He did as instructed, slowly turning around. A riot cop was training a gun on him. He hadn't even heard footsteps.

"What're you doing here?" the cop asked.

"I heard voices. No one's around, so—"

"Where have you been the past couple days?"

"In bed." The cop's eyebrows rose at that, so he added, "I've had a pretty rough weekend."

"I guess so." The cop's posture relaxed slightly as his eyes ran up and down Roddy. "Still better than most around here."

Roddy spared a glance toward Flint's. "I guess so."

"You've got an honest face," the cop said, seeming to thrust out his chest. "Saintly, even."

An odd comment to hear when Roddy was almost positive he still had some vomit crusted in one corner of his mouth. "Does that mean I'm free to go?"

The cop snorted a laugh. "I didn't say that."

"So you're going to shoot me?" Roddy looked down the barrel. Not what he'd have chosen for himself, but it could offer a quick end to this bizarre footnote on his death.

The cop pressed a finger to his ear. He was listening to someone else. That's when Roddy's eyes caught on the oddly-placed button on the cop's chest—except it wasn't a button. He had a body cam. He was showing Roddy to someone.

"Nope," the cop finally said, apparently at the whim of someone more important than himself. "No shooting today. I've got a more important job for you."

Part Two: Twenty-Two Years Later

Jules
New York City, New York – October 11ᵗʰ, 2084

"Since this is our last session together," Jules said, settling into her armchair and crossing her legs, "I want to open things up. Any concerns you have, anything that feels unfinished, it's all fair game."

Gwen sat across from Jules in her usual place on the couch. "I guess I'm feeling a little abandoned," she said, not meeting Jules' eyes. "I don't want to start a relationship with a new therapist, especially after getting this far with you."

Jules was getting this a lot. She should've been glad her clients didn't want her to leave, but instead, she entered every session with a rock in her stomach, dreading the moment she'd have to comfort them about a trauma of her own making.

"That's completely understandable," she said, "but it's important to remember this change isn't personal. It's an unfortunate reality that relationships, both professional and personal, sometimes end just because life takes you in two different directions."

She'd hoped Gwen would accept that answer and move on, but Gwen said nothing, her mouth set in a dissatisfied frown.

"Is there anything that makes you feel abandoned personally?" Jules prodded.

Gwen scraped her wine-colored thumbnail along a seam in the couch. "I don't understand why you're going."

"You're familiar with Rebirth?" It was a dumb question. Everyone who'd been to a church in the past twenty years knew Rebirth.

"Well, yeah, but I didn't think you were . . . one of those."

Jules caught herself raising an eyebrow and scratched her forehead to hide it. "One of what?"

"In some circles, the whole Rebirth thing is looked at as a little selfish."

That was a new one. Jules' friends and family had been praising her selflessness since she'd committed to making the sacrifice.

"Why would it be selfish?"

"A lot of people like to think their therapists care about helping them," Gwen said, a bitter note invading her voice. "When you need money and documented years in a service profession so you can do something for yourself, it feels . . . icky."

Jules schooled her features. "And you're one of these people that think Rebirth is icky?"

Gwen shrugged.

"Do you understand why someone might want it?" Jules asked.

"It's about being closer to God or something, right?"

"You're becoming as God-like as a human can be. The public service is part of it—you live a simple life helping others for years—but it's not like you go live in a palace after. You have to abandon your worldly possessions and experience Jesus' pain just to become Reborn. What comes after that is anyone's guess."

Gwen leaned forward, her voice lowering as if someone from the Church would overhear her. "It doesn't weird you out that no one's ever seen one of the Reborn after their ceremony?"

Her stomach fluttered at the thought. "It's not like they stop existing. There's housing for them."

"Right. They're just too good to interact with everyone else."

Jules paused, trying to separate herself from the conversation. Gwen felt betrayed, and her feelings were valid, even if she was inappropriately projecting her hurt and anger onto the Reborn.

"Is that why you think I'm leaving?" Jules asked, her voice level. "Because I think I'm too good for you?"

Gwen looked at the ceiling, her dark eyes filling with tears. "Maybe."

"Would it help to tell you what Rebirth means to me?"

"Maybe." A few of the tears leaked from the corners of Gwen's eyes, and she wiped them quickly, as if hoping Jules wouldn't notice.

"When I was little, I didn't really believe in God." Jules paused, letting her admission of heresy sink in.

"Were you raised by . . . you know." Gwen leaned forward, her voice a harsh whisper. "Atheists?"

Jules shook her head. "I went to church and prayed and all the normal stuff, but my heart wasn't in it."

"What happened?"

"Redemption. I saw the demon on TV with my own eyes. After that, everything we'd talked about in church all those years stopped feeling so hypothetical. I was glued to that screen the full twenty-four hours. When the Second Coming was announced, I might as well have been at the press conference."

Understanding dawned on Gwen's face. "So, when Rebirth became a thing . . ."

"It was the only future I could see for myself. I think it was God's way of telling me my purpose is to devote myself to His will, and His will is to help people. I truly believe that's what I'll be doing once I'm Reborn. Helping people—from out of sight, maybe, but only the truly selfish need credit for their deeds."

Gwen settled back into her seat, her eyes thoughtful but no longer watery. She offered Jules a polite smile. "I really hope you're right."

Rodrick

~~*Truth or Consequences*~~ *Redemption, New Mexico – October 11th, 2084*

Roddy only logged out on client days. Otherwise, he was patched in twenty-four seven. Why wouldn't he be when he lived in a ghost town? Today was a client day, though, so he pulled out his neural interface and took off the visor.

He showered—he needed to be presentable on client days—and then hopped into the car. With most of Redemption's population dead or relocated, he'd gotten his pick of the houses, and he'd chosen a big one on the edge of town, about as far away from the Chapel of the Reborn as he could get. Still, the drive wasn't long; Redemption was small, and ghost towns were great for traffic.

He made it to the chapel long before the client, as always. Punctuality was the price to pay for free neural interfacing. He could waste away in VR on his own time, but if he missed a client, it would be nothing but cold, hard reality for him, no filter.

He was in position behind the counter when the client walked in—an older guy in a threadbare suit, dark hair lightly dusted with gray. Small eyes peeking out from a bed of crow's feet swept the room, taking in its plainness. That always seemed to surprise them. They expected a traditional church with pews and an altar, maybe some stained glass. This was a small shop front with no wares, just a few paintings on the walls, single-pane windows of clear glass, and the big cross hanging behind the counter. The majority of the building's space was in the back, reserved for the people that paid.

"Welcome to the Chapel of the Reborn," Roddy said,

summoning the energy for fake cheerfulness. "Do you have an appointment?" He always asked, even though he only came to the chapel if he was expecting someone.

The man nodded, gravitating toward the counter. "Ed Sheppard."

Roddy double-checked the name, but he already knew it was right. "Excellent. Congratulations on making the life-changing decision to be Reborn. I'll take your photo ID and donation now, and then we can get started."

The man hesitated. They often did. Giving up your life savings all in one go wasn't a natural choice for anyone, even if they'd planned for it all their life. He produced his ID first, then slowly pulled an envelope out of his coat pocket and laid it on the counter.

Roddy counted it in front of Ed. It was over the mandatory minimum donation, but not by much. He tucked the cash safely away in the vault, then walked around the counter. "This way," he said, waving Ed along toward the corner. The counter ended just before a space with a locked door. Roddy pulled his jangling key set from his belt and let them inside.

"This is where the magic happens, eh?" Ed said.

Roddy'd heard that one before. Once, he'd quipped that there was no place for magic in Christianity, but that client had looked about to shit himself with nerves. Roddy had tried harder not to freak clients out after that. It was the least he could do.

He smiled at Ed. "Sure is." Then, he led Ed to the corner where the VR assembly rested on the floor. "Have a seat," he said, gesturing to the linoleum.

Ed glanced at Roddy, clearly thrown off by the lack of furniture.

"It's more comfortable than what Jesus had," Roddy said.

Ed sat. He'd made his point.

"Ever use one of these before?" Roddy asked.

Usually, the answer was no—Rebirth took some extreme saving, and neural interfacing wasn't cheap. Still, Roddy sometimes got rich people who'd decided to sacrifice it all, or more commonly, people with rich friends.

Ed must have been one of the above, because he nodded. "I've got a port," he said, tapping his left temple.

"Great," Roddy said, holding out the visor.

As he took it, Ed jerked his head toward the other side of the room. A metal door fit snugly into the back wall. "Is that for after?"

"You guessed it." Roddy was relieved that, with the way Ed had worded the question, he didn't have to lie.

Once Ed got his visor situated, Roddy connected the neural interface. "I'm turning it on now. Are you ready?"

"Is there anything in particular I'm supposed to do?" Anxiety raised Ed's voice a note higher.

Roddy touched Ed's shoulder for reassurance, knowing he could no longer see through the visor. "Nothing you can do will change what happens."

Ed nodded, the tension in his shoulders easing slightly, and Roddy flipped the switch that turned on the VR set-up. When everything was running as intended, he slipped quietly out the way he came in. Back in the front room, he eased the giant cross down from the wall and slipped it into the unobtrusive brackets on either side of the door to bar Ed inside. Only once he'd finished did he slip a hand under the counter and press the button concealed there, the one that previous owners of the building would have called the panic button. In his head, Roddy called it that, still. Someone would be panicking, anyway.

Jules

New York City, New York to Redemption, New Mexico –
October 15th and 16th, 2084

Jules flew from LaGuardia to Roswell, where she stayed in a hotel for the first time in her adult life. That night, as she sank into the hot tub, she contemplated the irony that her trip to Redemption had exposed her to such luxury. Perhaps it was built-in, the idea that traveling would remind you of exactly what you were giving up. God's final test. How many people just wrapped themselves in plush hotel bathrobes and ordered a plane ticket home?

It didn't matter. That wouldn't be her.

The next day, she spent four hours in the back of a cab, watching the scrublands go by and the meter tick upward. She'd never burned through money like this in her life, but it was okay. This was the trip she'd saved it all for.

Eventually, the cab pulled into an empty little town. She knew it was Redemption without reading the signs. It had been decades since the demon had roamed these streets on her TV, but she could've sworn she recognized some of the buildings like she'd just seen them that morning.

She paid the cabbie and stepped out onto the cracked sidewalk. Her legs shook. She was finally here, and it was like nothing she'd ever experienced. New Yorkers expected people everywhere, even in the middle of the night, but here, it was mid-afternoon and the only movement in sight was the cab quickly becoming a yellow glint in the distance. For a moment, she wanted to call out to it, to wave her arms and beg it to come back because it felt so wrong to intrude on this silence. Instead, she took a step forward, and the sign for the chapel caught her eye.

It looked like a real body hanging from a horizontal pole above the street, its arms nailed in T-formation while its legs dangled uselessly beneath. Jules poured over the details, from the pained expression to the long, greasy hair anointed with a crown of thorns. Red paint even ran like blood. This sign decorated the cover of all the chapel's pamphlets, including the one Jules kept tacked to her bedroom wall through most of her teenage years. She could barely believe she was seeing it in person after looking at that picture every single day. It felt almost like stepping into a world she'd visited in dreams but had never known to be real.

Once she'd admired every brushstroke of the sign, she let herself inside. The front room of the chapel was perfectly under-stated, just rustic wooden walls with paintings chosen to remind you why you'd come. A man stood behind the plain wooden counter, and He looked so much like the sign out front that Jules would have believed He'd just climbed down and hung up His crown on the way in. He could be no one else but Rod.

She frantically searched her memory—surely somewhere in the literature, they'd taught her the proper way to greet Rod if she met Him—but He saved her the need to embarrass herself by speaking first.

"Welcome to the Chapel of the Reborn. Do you have an appointment?"

Rod was talking to her.

"Yes. I was told to be here at two o'clock. Jules Thomas?"

He skimmed a list in the book in front of Him. How many people came to be Reborn? It was hard to get a sense of the numbers when the Reborn didn't remain in society's eye afterward.

He tapped the list. "There you are. Excellent. Congratulations on making the life-changing decision to be Reborn. I'll take your photo ID and donation now, and then we can get started."

"Of course." Her hands shook. Had she remembered her photo ID? Of course she had. She'd used it for the plane and the hotel, and besides, she never left her apartment without it. Still, that trickle of panic didn't subside until she held it in her hands. Funny how all logic went out the window when you were faced with something you wanted so badly to change your life.

"Here." She gave Him the ID and money and waited while He counted it out.

A giant cross, made of the same wood as the wall, hung behind Him in a place of almost threatening prominence. This was only supposed to be a crucifixion simulation, right? She studied it casually for bloodstains but saw none. She shook her head. Trust the process.

"This all looks good," Rod said, handing her ID back and tucking the money out of sight behind the counter.

"Do you need a record of how it was earned?" she asked. "My service history?"

"You should have sent all that ahead through the application online."

"Oh. Right." Nerves again. "Do people make idiots of themselves here a lot?"

He smiled. "You're not an idiot. It's just a big day."

She took a deep breath. She'd come here to experience His ancient pain, but here He was, comforting her. A painting on the wall caught her eye—Rod, standing between the demon and the road out of Redemption. He held a small cross up to the demon, symbolic of the fact that He was about to vanquish it back to Hell. The title of the painting hung beneath it: "The Second Coming."

"I watched all the coverage back in the day," she said, nodding toward the painting. "I guess most people you get in here did, but I was a kid. I didn't even really believe before the demon came."

"Really?" A spark of something lit in His eyes. Likely, He loved hearing about all the souls He'd saved.

"I wish they'd gotten footage of the moment you showed up. I know cameras can't be everywhere—maybe miracles don't even show up on tape—but it would have been nice to see it in more than just paintings."

"What kept you from believing before then?" He asked.

Two minutes ago, she'd have panicked, thinking this was some test she'd set herself up to fail, but with the easy way Rod leaned on the counter looking at her, she didn't feel like she was being examined. She felt heard.

"I always believed what I could see with my eyes or feel with my hands," she said. "Not very Christian of me, but I guess I needed a little taste of Heaven and Hell in the real world before I could believe the Bible wasn't just full of stories."

Rod nodded, but His smile dropped away. Maybe she should've worried.

"Since then, I try to use it as an example to inspire my clients," she added to change the focus.

"Remind me, what do you do again?"

Her heart took a momentary dive, but that was stupid. With as many people surely came for Rebirth, she couldn't expect Him to remember everything about her application. That would be hubris.

"I'm a therapist. A lot of my clients suffer from depression and suicidal ideation, and they feel about their future the same way I felt about God. They think because they've never seen life get better, it never will. The concept doesn't exist for them."

"And you make them see it?"

"I try."

"Now that is godly work."

"Not like yours." She looked away, hoping He wouldn't notice the blush climbing her cheeks.

He sighed and stepped around the counter. "Definitely not like mine."

Rodrick
Redemption, New Mexico – October 16th, 2084

This was why Roddy tried not to engage with his clients; he got too attached. He needed these people to be empty faces, mindless drones he could look down on for believing propaganda. But this girl wasn't stupid. She'd questioned the religion being shoved down her throat until she saw what she thought was proof on TV. Even now that she believed, she was using her belief to save lives. It was the sort of thing most Christians only pretended they would do.

If he'd had a therapist like her back in the day, maybe he

wouldn't have downed those pills. Of course, he probably would have been eaten, instead, but at least then, he wouldn't be in this mess.

Hesitantly, he unlocked the door and led her to the VR assembly. Struck by newfound empathy, he saw the room the way she must have: unsettlingly empty. The reinforced metal door opposite the entrance glistened prominently against the otherwise old-fashioned walls. Still, he forced himself to follow his script. "Have a seat."

Jules sat without comment. She didn't see herself as too good for the floor. In fact, she hardly had eyes for anything but the VR visor.

"Ever use one of these before?" Roddy asked.

She shook her head. "But I always wanted to."

"Yeah?" That wasn't a comment he got often; most aspiring Reborn didn't admit to being tempted by pure entertainment.

Her lips twisted into an embarrassed smile. "I loved video games as a kid. I was more into controller games than VR, but when they invented the neural interface . . . it would be cool to know what it really feels like to *be* your character for once." She shrugged dismissively. "Now, I guess I'll find out."

So she needed a port. Damn. He wanted this over with before he did something he'd regret. "Since you've never used a neural interface, you need a port drilled for proper access, or the simulation won't be able to engage your non-sight senses."

Her eyes met his. "So we can't move forward?"

"I'm trained. It's a simple procedure once you've learned it. Stay here. I'll be right back." He ducked out of the room to fetch his drill kit from behind the counter.

"What kinds of video games did you play?" he asked as he slipped back into the room with the tools. As much as he tried to avoid unnecessary engagement, he always asked questions when drilling a port. A distraction kept people from getting too scared, and everyone seemed the most distracted when they talked about themselves.

"Action-adventure, mostly," she said. "I liked having a mission to carry out."

He knelt beside her, laying out his tools. "Everyone needs purpose. Did you have a favorite game?"

She barely had to think before speaking. "Cosmic Warfare II. But I quit gaming around the time the Chapel of the Reborn opened up."

"What was it about?" He sized up his drill bits, comparing them to the side of her head.

"Aliens."

The drill bit slipped from his fingers, clinking gently as it bounced across the empty room. "Aliens?"

"Dumb, I know," she said, her face closing up. "Kid stuff." She must have picked up on his surprise—of course a therapist would—and misinterpreted the reason for it.

"Not at all," he said, retrieving the bit. "Tell me more."

She smiled hesitantly and continued. "I actually believed in them back then. There were all these stories of people seeing them and being abducted. There was also supposed to be some government program revolving around reverse-engineering their technology pre-Unity. I used to think it still existed and was being covered up since it didn't fit the Church's official stance on things. Looking back, it was probably wishful thinking, because I always wanted to be like my character in the game."

She'd believed in aliens? Roddy hadn't thought anyone alive in his lifetime still believed in aliens. He fiddled with the drill bits, comparing a few despite having already decided which would fit her head. "Who was the character?"

"Ava Shadow. She was really tough and super smart. Basically the person every middle school girl wanted to be, at least if they were anything like me."

Ava Shadow. That actually sounded familiar. Hadn't he seen that character in the VR-verse? Maybe Jules could still know what it would feel like to play her with a neural interface—except she couldn't, because she was here, and she wouldn't be able to play anything when he'd finished with her.

Abandoning the drill bits, he drew up a few mLs of local anesthetic. Just one little sting and she'd be ready for the port. She straightened her head, actually trying to make it easier for him, and her auburn hair slipped down in front of her temple. He moved to brush it back but paused with it in his hand. Its red tint reminded him of Jan, and for a moment, he slipped back in time, watching the lights glisten off Jan's hair on the last night he'd ever seen her—the last night she'd been seen at all. So many had disappeared that weekend; the government only confirmed death if remains could be found, and for the majority of victims, that would never happen. Still, it hadn't taken long for Roddy to assume the worst. Maybe she was out there somewhere, flying under his radar, happy to let him think she'd died to avoid any more potential arguments. Maybe, but he didn't believe it.

This woman, though. This ex-gamer who used her beliefs to save people that didn't think they were worth saving. She was alive, completely and utterly, and she still had most of her life ahead of her. If that changed, it would be because of Roddy. He'd done enough unspeakable things in his life that if hell didn't already exist, one might be created just for him, but it was never too late to try to be better.

He leaned forward, and instead of sinking the needle into her flesh, he whispered, "Get out while you can."

She turned sharply to look at him, pricking her cheek and jerking away. "What?" she asked, wincing.

He withdrew the syringe and recapped it. "Rebirth isn't real."

"Is this a test?"

"No. I swear to you. Whatever you think you know about Redemption, that's not how it went down."

"And you want me to know the truth? Is this part of the process?"

"There is no process. It's all bullshit."

"What do you mean?"

"I'm not the Second Coming. I'm just some guy with long hair who was in the right place at the right time."

She rose up on her knees, facing him. "That can't be true. You're testing me. I saw it with my own eyes. There was a demon."

"No, you saw it on TV, and they told you there was a demon. I don't think that's what it is."

"What was it, then?"

"No one's ever told me, but I've heard some things. I think it's an alien."

Her eyes flew wide. "What?"

"Like in your game."

"No." She shook her head violently, like she could fling the concept right out of her brain. "Aliens aren't real. And why would one be here? That doesn't make sense."

"There's a lot of nothing out here," he said, gesturing vaguely in a way he hoped suggested the desert outside. "Maybe you've noticed? Plenty of space for the government to hide stuff, including aliens it's studying."

"Aliens aren't real," she said again, more firmly. "The Church says so. Why would they tell us that if they knew it was wrong?"

Roddy shrugged. "Let's say the stuff you read about as a kid was true. There was some secret program to study aliens—not just their technology but aliens themselves. Then Unity happened. The Church and the government combined, and they each got access to each other's deep, dark secrets. The Church might let the experiments continue, but there's no way they'd suddenly announce, 'Just kidding. Aliens are real, after all. Don't ask us how we know.' If anything, they'd double down in the other direction, just to cover their tracks."

Jules frowned as she listened, and Roddy remembered his countless debates with Jan. No matter how strong his argument was, her belief was always stronger. Would that be the case with Jules, too, or did she still have that questioning little girl inside her somewhere?

"If that's true," she said, her voice tentative, "what happened here in Redemption? Where did this whole Rebirth thing come from?"

"From what I can put together, the alien got loose and massacred the town. Ate everyone. Maybe it was some kind of predator naturally, or maybe they did something to it. I don't know, but it sure seems drawn to human flesh in particular. Regardless, they didn't want to admit they were responsible, so they called it a demon, and who better to claim got rid of a demon than Jesus Christ reincarnated?" He spread out his arms to indicate himself.

"So you're not . . ."

"Nope."

"And you didn't really vanquish it?"

"No one did." He shot a meaningful glance at the door across the room. "It's still here."

"What?" She paled a little as she stared at the door. At least she seemed to believe him.

"I don't know if they couldn't kill it or just didn't want to, but they trapped it here, changed the name of the town, and made up Rebirth. It's all a gimmick. People spend their lives in service positions just to give all their money to the Church when they're done. They waltz right into town of their own volition and tie up their own loose ends by telling their families they're off to be Reborn and will never see them again."

"Loose ends?" Jules asked, not getting it.

He couldn't look at her. "Alien's gotta eat."

She jumped to her feet. He followed suit, though more slowly.

"You're telling me you've been masquerading as Christ himself when really, you've been feeding innocent people to a monster?"

"I didn't exactly get a choice, but yeah."

Her eyes found his and smoldered. "There's always a choice."

He turned back the way they'd come. "I'm not expecting you to forgive me, but my bosses check in pretty regularly. We don't have much time if we're gonna get you out of here."

He opened the door leading back into the storefront but stopped when he realized she wasn't following. He turned. She was edging toward the reinforced door, his drill held in front of her like a gun.

"What are you doing?" he asked.

"If what you said was true, I can't let this go on. I need to kill it."

He crossed back to her, putting a staying hand on her arm. "It'll kill you. You won't stand a chance."

Unshed tears glistened in her eyes. "Then I'll go down knowing I tried to do what was right."

"Get out of here. Live your life. If anyone should die trying to kill it, it's me." He didn't plan on living with himself after this, anyway.

"What life?" She made a sound halfway between a laugh and a sob. "Everything I've lived for since I was a kid is a lie. Like you said, I tied up my loose ends. I have nothing to go home to."

Roddy saw himself in her steely expression and wondered at the irony. He'd lived a life of sin while she'd lived a life of service, yet this world had brought them both here. How fitting would it be if the Church were taken down by the people its own hands had hollowed out?

Still, there was more than one way to revolt.

His hand slid down her arm to rest on the drill, directing it at the floor.

"What about your clients?" he said.

Her hard expression faltered just slightly before settling back into place. "I said my goodbyes."

"I'm sure you did, but do you really think none of them still need you? There wasn't exactly an overabundance of good thera-pists before Redemption. I doubt that's changed much, even with Rebirth as an incentive."

She stared down at the drill, her eyes far away. "What makes you think I was a good therapist?"

"Well, you showed up here, and all the sudden, you've got me wanting to break the system I've been enabling for the past twenty years."

"I get the sense you've always wanted to. You just didn't feel like you could."

"See what I mean? And you want to throw those skills away on this?" He jerked his head toward the drill.

"I'm not throwing them away if what I'm dying for is important. We need to at least try to put a stop to this."

"We will, but hear me out. We can't get to the alien if we're both in here. The door doesn't exactly have a knob. Someone has to go open it."

"So go open it and come back—"

"Someone also has to bar the door."

Her forehead crinkled. "What? Why?"

"Because if it kills us and that door's not barred, there'll be another massacre. Only this time, it'll be our fault."

"What happens to the person on the outside, then?"

"If it's me, the Church tracks me down and has me killed, then comes up with some story to make me a martyr. They'll kill you, too, if the alien doesn't do it for them. But if it's you on the outside, you can run. If anyone asks, you got as far as your last hotel and changed your mind, decided Rebirth wasn't for you. It happens often enough."

"I can't just walk away and leave you to die."

"It's easier than you'd think."

Her eyes darted to him, and he used the moment to fully yank the drill from her hand.

"At least you have my consent," he said. "Come on. I'll show you what to do." He returned to the front room, trying to hide his surprise when she followed him. "I use the big cross to bar the door." He set the drill aside to lift the cross off the wall and prop it against the end of the counter. "It's kind of heavy, but I think you can lift it. Want to try?"

She stared at him.

He sighed. "I decided my fate the moment I started considering this. Don't let them have us both."

Hesitantly, she stepped forward, lifted the cross, and set it back down. "I can do it," she said quietly.

He nodded. "Just fit it into these," he said, tapping the brackets on either side of the door. His heart started to pound. He'd never imagined teaching someone how to murder him. "Once it's secure, press this little button." He stepped behind the counter and pointed. "Then, get out of here as fast as you can." He pulled her money back out of the vault and handed it to her, then went to the book and scribbled *NO SHOW* next to her name. When he finished, she was still staring at the wad of cash in her hand. "Jules?"

"Do you know how many times I went without so I could put this money away?" she asked, her voice thin. "How hard I worked as a therapist so I could give my life to God? Only, now that I'm finally here, I find out there's no trace of him in this wasteland. There never was."

"Who needs him? Did you like being a therapist?"

"Yeah, but—"

"Then take that money, buy yourself a ticket home, and get

your clients back. Be a therapist because you want to help people, not because some god told you to."

She looked from him back down to the money in her fist, then gave a small nod. "Thank you."

"Now, we need to hurry if we're going to get you out of here before anyone shows up." He picked up the drill and held it high, as if he would really have a chance in there. Might as well give her hope.

He stepped into the room where he'd sent countless others to their deaths. Lightheaded, he closed his eyes and took a deep breath. Then, he turned toward Jules, who stood in the doorway. Sunlight beamed in through the window behind her, lighting up the edges of her Jan-red hair.

"Whenever you're ready," he said.

"You tear that thing apart."

He attempted a smile. "Will do."

She shut the door, closing out the sunlight and leaving him with the weak illumination of the overhead bulb. In a moment, a dull scraping sound spoke of the cross, his crucifix, being heaved into place. When it stopped, all he could hear was his heartbeat. He waited.

With a groan, the metal door opened.

Jules
New York City, New York – October 25th, 2084

Jules had anticipated that many of her clients would refuse to come back to her services. After all, she'd shown her willingness to abandon them. Most relationships didn't survive that. Those who did want her back were mostly the clients that claimed aspirations of Rebirth themselves but had never gotten around to doing anything about it. She supposed those were the people who both understood why she had left and could imagine reasons why, in the end, she might have come back.

Gwen had never seemed well-disposed to the idea of Rebirth, so Jules was particularly surprised when she wanted to jump right back into her old appointment schedule as though nothing had changed. Still, an awkwardness hung between them as they settled into their well-worn positions across from each other for the first time since Jules had returned.

"How have things been these past two weeks?" Jules asked. It was an opening question she used often.

Gwen hesitated a moment before speaking. "I've been thinking a lot about my faith."

"Your faith?"

She shifted in her seat. "If I tell you a secret, will it stay in this room, no matter what?"

"As long as you don't intend to hurt yourself or others, I'm not obligated to report anything you say to anyone." Jules leaned slightly forward. "What is it?"

"I've never really . . . *believed.* I go to church and everything, but I figured the actual stories in the Bible—even the existence of God, to an extent—was meant to be more metaphorical. I thought most people felt that way. But when you told me about your relationship with Rebirth, I realized I was wrong. People were supposed to literally believe this stuff. First, I worried somebody was going to catch me, even though all this was going on inside my head, but then I wondered if maybe I'd been wrong." Gwen focused her eyes on Jules. "And then you came back. If you couldn't go through with it, I really don't know what to think."

"I see," Jules said.

The confession was huge. Other therapists had reported clients for less. Gwen must have really trusted Jules to admit this to her—or at least, she trusted the idea that if Jules was having a religious crisis, she wouldn't condemn Gwen for hers.

"I thought maybe, if you told me why you changed your mind about Rebirth, it could help me straighten out my own thoughts," Gwen continued.

I decided I could serve God best by staying here with my clients. That was the proper answer, the one she'd given the government official who'd stopped by late the previous week with questions about why she'd never shown up for her Rebirth.

Of course, he hadn't mentioned Rod. Neither had the news. She'd expected to hear something, either a story glorifying Rod's death or announcing that the Church of the Reborn had been shut down, but no. As far as the rest of the world could tell, nothing unusual had happened in that Church last week. Rod's true sacrifice—for surely, that's what it was in the end—was lost forever in the shadows of history.

Unless she helped it live on. She could still remember the feel of the drill in her hand, the certainty that she'd found a cause worth more than her life. Rod's death was an act of rebellion as much as of kindness, but true rebellion didn't end with one man. Not when others who believed in it still drew breath.

Jules set her notepad aside and settled back into her chair. "Let me tell you some things about Rebirth."

THE DEVIL YOU DON'T KNOW

DEVIN HUNT

The first case solved by HANK FREDRICKS, P.I. and Associates

The sound of the gunshot seems unimportant at first, and the tug at Hank's back is more annoying than painful.

Two steps later, he stumbles and falls forward. Blood pools on the warehouse floor.

"Not much of a rescue," Hank says, pawing at the bullet hole in his abdomen.

* * *

Sent by: Renee Ducette <rducette@dkopartners.org> Fri. Apr. 28, 2023. Today, 4:15pm

To: Hank Fredricks <hfredricks@dkopartners.org>

It's nothing that couldn't wait till Monday, but Accounting flagged the 'V.F. and Associates' account. V.F. & A haven't asked for almost anything since grandpa Ducette's day but never stopped paying their annual retainer. Accounting says if we had something with a real person's signature on it, it would look a lot less like a money laundering scheme. Someone can fake a faxed signature, so we need you to watch a real person sign something, anything. Free Monday?

Renee Ducette,

Partner at the law offices of Ducette, Kopley and Olsen

Sent by: Hank Fredricks <hfredricks@dkopartners.org> Fri. Apr. 28, 2023. Today, 4:32 pm

To: Renee Ducette <rducette@dkopartners.org>

I just looked into them. They've had the same mailing address, down the street from the Empire State Building, for <u>100 years</u>. Apparently this firm helped them buy the building in 1924, but the name on the account back then was 'V. Frankenstein'? Weird, right?

Monday: free

Actual person: check.

P.S. Did any of your cop buddies get back to you on those murders around the corner?

Hank Fredricks,

Investigator at the law offices of Ducette, Kopley and Olsen

Sent by: Renee Ducette <rducette@dkopartners.org> Fri. Apr.

28, 2023. Today, 4:40pm

> To: Hank Fredricks <hfredricks@dkopartners.org>

> Thanks in advance, Hank! Enjoy your weekend and give Dani my best.

> P.S. They still don't have anything more than the pictures I sent you of the crime scenes. They continue to recommend 'avoiding the area'.

> Renee Ducette,
> Partner at the law offices of Ducette, Kopley and Olsen

Hank Fredricks throws on his coat without responding. If "V.F. and Associates" were doing something illegal, he wanted to know it *before* he walked in on Monday asking questions.

* * *

Hank sips coffee as he stakes out the office building from the overpriced Midtown coffee shop across the street. Hank likes stakeouts in coffee shops: a clean-shaven man with quietly expensive clothes and gray-streaked hair can stay warm and unmolested for hours. Afternoon fades to dusk, and booths full of parents with children give way to college students writing and cramming.

Hank finally covers his mug when they come to refill it, checking his notes one last time: the building where the letters get delivered is six stories, tall for the 1920s when they built it, rumored to have been a speakeasy. The building is zoned commercial on the bottom four floors and residential for the top two. All mail comes and goes from office 421, which records say is in the northeast corner of the fourth floor. He glances up one last time, hoping the notes will spark something.

All the offices in the building, except that one, have gone dark

A thin line of light shines around thick curtains: someone is there late

It would be an unnecessary liability to use a fake address full of real people

Verdict: probably safe to go in on Monday.

But as Hank rises to leave, the curtains part, revealing a broad figure who opens the window. It stands aside.

And something *massive* spreads its wings and flaps out into the night.

"Holy shit!" Hank hisses to himself. The neighboring table looks his way and Hank waves sheepishly. "Sorry . . . just a bird . . ."

The students go back to their laptops and their cups of dark propellant.

Hank pays the barista—or baristo, Hank's not sure what you call a young guy serving coffee in a place this pretentious—and hustles out. He doesn't want Dani worrying that he's late. He hasn't taken three steps down the sidewalk before he bumps into a man wearing a strange white hat, staring up at the buildings like a tourist and talking on his phone. The man curses in what's probably German as Hank hurries home.

* * *

"What's the biggest bird you've seen in the city?" Hank asks Dani as they sit down for dinner, scooping beef stroganoff out of a skillet.

"Biggest bird . . . there're these seagulls down at the docks,

44

'great black-backed gulls' and, well, they live up to the name; they're humongous." She holds out her hands as wide as they go. "With black backs. Why?"

"Hmm . . . Probably big enough," he muses, "I saw a bird tonight, but the wings were probably too wide to have been a gull,"

She pokes him in the arm. "Does Renee know you're spending the firm's money *birdwatching*?"

"I wasn't! It flew out the window of an office I was watching."

"An *office?*" she sputters. "Where?"

"Midtown. Someone working late set it free, maybe?"

"Probably an exotic pet that got too big for an apartment, or it could be you're starting to see things in your old age," she teases, grinning over her glasses.

"*Me? Old?* I thought I was going to live forever!"

* * *

Monday morning, paperwork in hand, Hank enters the building owned by V. F. and Associates, opting for the stairs over an untrustworthy ancient elevator. In the farthest corner of the fourth floor, their office door reads '421' in art nouveau gold lettering on a blacked-out window. When Hank knocks, nobody answers, despite it being well into Monday morning. Extra curious since someone was *definitely* here late on Friday. Good mysteries are rare in a lawyer's office, and this was the first one in years. He had to admit that the steady check was nice, but he missed real P.I. work.

Time for Plan B. Inside the only occupied office bordering 421, Hank finds an interior designer whose business is new and who is more than happy to entertain an interested stranger. Hank doesn't say that he's a potential client, but he lets the guy imagine he might be. Hank moves about the office, complimenting the bold choices and clean lines. The young designer offers him coffee, and once he leaves to get it, Hank slips out an open window onto the wrought iron fire escape clinging to the outside of the building.

Hank tries not to look down as he moves to the window that the giant bird left through on Friday. The window, though ajar, barely budges when Hank pulls on it, and he has to use his full strength to open a big enough gap to slide through.

Is he getting old? He saw someone open it so easily on Friday. He won't get any answers to his growing pile of questions out here.

He slips inside.

Austere room, dominated by one massive ornate desk, giving more the impression of a private study than 'office space'

One parrot stand, but no other evidence of any birds

Two empty but dirty soup bowls, both decorated, not purely functional

The dried soup at the edges isn't three days old: people were here over the weekend

Verdict: Someone lives here, someone whose signature he needs.

With his pile of questions becoming mountainous, Hank creeps through an open door into a tall octagonal atrium with white marble floors and walls. Sunlight warms the space as it filters through the frosted glass ceiling two stories above. The centerpiece of the room is a freestanding spiral staircase rising two floors.

And sliding down the balustrade is the Devil himself.

He lands on two bare feet not five paces away and lowers his horns. Hank tries to stuff down his rising panic. He needs to focus.

"You angling to die?" the creature says, pawing at the ground.

Hank puts his hands out wide. He doesn't carry a gun anymore, but almost—almost—wishes he still did. With his adrenaline spiking, Hank takes in the satyr-devil.

Humanoid, a goat head on a thick neck, one horizontal pupil fixed on him

From the neck down, more like a chimpanzee or gorilla than a man

Black fur, thick arms ending in four-fingered hands: thumbs, no pinkies

A bulging tan sash wrapped across one shoulder: contents unclear
Monochrome gray t-shirt, tough canvas work pants, no shoes
Wide-set furry feet, each with a thumb
The Devil's bare feet seem familiar with the polished-smooth floor
Too many unknown variables to let this degenerate into a fight
Verdict: talk your way out of this.

"Easy now. Your lawyers sent me. I'm Hank Fredricks from Ducette, Kopley and Olsen. I have some papers I need you—or someone–to sign," he says, slowly gesturing to the papers in his pocket.

Something is *going on here, but it's not money laundering.*

A second voice echoes from the top of the stairs, but Hank doesn't dare take his eyes off the danger in front of him. "Scuff, I don't think this man is likely to be responsible for our friend's continued absence."

"Then why is he here?" the Devil—'Scuff,' apparently—replies, not looking away from Hank either.

The owner of the second voice comes into view as a truly massive man descends the stairs. His bright, high tenor calms Scuff, who straightens into a less violent posture. Hank tentatively lowers his arms.

The man's smiling face is a patchwork of old, stitched scars, a pattern that extends down his neck and even onto his hands where they aren't hidden by the sleeves of his suit jacket. His matching trousers are well-fitting; everything looks tailored (Hank imagines nothing his size is in stock at Macy's).

The scarred man towers over his infernal sentinel and places a gentle hand on the furry shoulder. Scuff leans into the touch, a strangely tender and childlike gesture from a monster who just threatened Hank with murder. Scuff's attention still follows Hank, the expression on the goat's face with its horizontally pupiled eye is unreadable, except for obvious hostility.

The giant squeezes Scuff's shoulder affectionately. "You must forgive Scuff. Surprises are so often dangerous, and he only wants to keep us safe. You must understand that you appearing here like this most certainly qualifies as a surprise."

"Sorry . . ." Hank shakes his head slightly, helping him refocus on his task, his ticket back out of here. "Uh . . . my name is Hank Fredricks, here on behalf of Ducette, Kopley and Olsen."

"Yes, I recall," the giant replies calmly.

Hank soldiers on, forcing his hands not to shake as he offers the paperwork. "I-I have some paperwork for someone to sign."

"I could have replied by mail, as I have for the last hundred years. You have very enterprisingly come so far as to enter our home."

The welcoming expression slips just slightly and is swiftly replaced. Hank has been in the game too long to miss danger hiding behind a smile; this man might be just as willing to kill.

"You must be, uh... 'V. F.' or an associate?" Hank asks, tightly controlling his voice to keep from stammering.

"Forgive my manners." The stitched giant beams. "My name is Victor Frankenstein II. You have no doubt heard of my 'father,' though little in those stories is true." He spreads his arms wide, showing himself off with a wink. "My first friend told me that I should carry my father's name, maybe find some redemption for the both of us. You may call me Victor. With introductions behind us, I ask once again: why are you *really* here?"

"Because . . . I saw something huge fly out your window this past Friday." It sounds so silly and small a reason now that he's saying it out loud. "Uh . . . sir." Hank can't bring himself to say 'Frankenstein,' as if saying it would admit that he *believed* he could be facing the fictional monster. That would be crazy, and Hank wasn't crazy.

The creatures exchange knowing glances before Victor breaks the silence. "So the reason you're here is that you were snooping and couldn't help but snoop a little more. I suppose I can forgive you a little home invasion. Are you not a professional snoop? Irrepressible curiosity: professional hazard, et cetera, et cetera?"

"I'm an investigator, so . . . yeah." Hank shrugs, he hopes disarmingly.

"Friday, Father!" Scuff presses. "He said he saw Ariel on *Friday!*"

"He did, indeed," the giant agrees.

"What did you do with Ariel?" Scuff accuses.

"'Do with Ariel'?" Hank retorts. "Nothing! I only saw it for a second before I lost it in the dark-"

"'Him,' not 'it'!" Scuff surges forward, twisting his head to present his horns, one broken, the other spiraling a foot longer into a lethal spear. He is restrained in a flash by the hand of the giant, the monster—Frankenstein's monster, Victor Frankenstein II.

"Investigator Fredricks. As startling as you may find our appearance, *never* describe anyone here as '*it*.'" Frankenstein's eyes are hard. Hank swears he sees lightning flash across them.

"It won't happen again." Hank manages not to stammer.

"So what did you see? What direction did you see our friend fly?" Victor asks.

"North? I didn't get a great look at . . . *him,*" Hank says carefully.

A third voice—small, pensive and slow—drawls, "So, Central Park, as he'd suggested. He'd hoped to hang from the angel's wings."

Seeing no one move, Hank searches for the source of the small voice.

The new voice chuckles as Hank fails to find its origin. Three long, curved claws emerge from the baby-sling around Scruff's barrel chest and *wave* to Fredericks before catching the edge and pulling it down to reveal the face of a . . . fuzzy baby? No, a *sloth.* With a neatly buttoned suit-vest and a *tie.*

"The trail is three days cold and getting colder!" Scuff growls down at the small creature. "He's never been gone this long. If he was lost or hurt, someone would have seen him by now, and it would have made the news!"

"Perhaps . . . and perhaps the sudden appearance of a professional snoop isn't the disaster it looks like," Victor muses aloud. "You see, Investigator Fredricks, while we might cause alarm walking down the street, you wouldn't get a second look. Would you look where we cannot and find our missing friend?"

"I–I'm sorry, I don't do private work anymore. I'm afraid

I can't help you . . . uh, Sir." Victor Frankenstein II smirks at the honorific.

Hank would have agreed to almost anything to get back into private investigating work or out of this office, but not . . . this, with . . . *these.*

After a concerning pause, during which where Hank worries he might never be getting out of here, Frankenstein's countenance brightens. He says, "I understand," as if he hadn't a care in the world. "In any event, I will take the paperwork. If you have gone to the trouble of delivering it in the face of obstacles, it must be rather urgent indeed, so let us not delay its return any further. Would you care to step into my office?" Frankenstein gestures back the way Hank had come. Scuff takes his leave, wordlessly stomping up the steps.

The desk's massive size makes more sense with Victor behind it. The giant takes the papers and reads them, eyes darting with uncanny speed, and signs them in a matter of seconds.

With their business concluded, Victor offers his hand. Hank shakes it, hiding his reluctance to touch the creature. Hank's whole arm comes alive with a tingling, electric sensation he can't name, like feeling returning to a sleeping limb, but wonderful.

"It's been a pleasure, Investigator Hank Fredricks."

"You, too, uh, Victor Frankenstein."

Crazy. He's gone crazy.

* * *

Hank half runs back to Ducette, Kopley and Olsen. He drops off the paperwork with the receptionist, walks as calmly as he can back to his office, and locks the door behind him.

The 'alcoholic investigators' cliché doesn't stop him from

opening his little office bar and pouring himself a glass of brown. And then another. His hands start to shake, which hasn't happened in years.

The alcohol droplets glisten as they slide down the inside of the glass. He isn't sure how long he watches them.

* * *

Hank is startled back to reality as the phone rings. "H-Hank Fredricks, Investigations Department for Ducette, Kopley and Olsen."

"Yeah, I would hope so." Renee Ducette laughs. "Can you come to my office?"

"Sure, Renee, be right up." He pops a breath mint and heads upstairs.

When Hank knocks on the door to Renee's office, Renee, on the phone, silently beckons him in.

"Yes ... Mr. Fredricks just arrived ... Yes, that sounds very doable ... A week seems like you may be underestimating him ..." Renee seems relaxed, but Hank's unease grows word by word. "An NDA? That seems like overkill. Client confidentiality is ironclad, and in a town this small," Renee smirks, looking out at the New York City skyline, "trust is everything ... Oh, I see ... Yes, the fax is coming in now ... I'll tell him ... Oh, I *see* ... I'll transfer you to accounting. It was so nice to hear from you." Renee presses a few buttons on the phone and hangs up.

"A non-disclosure agreement? What was that all about?" Hank asks, but he's nervous he already knows the answer.

"Thanks for coming," Renee says. "I'm assured it's absolutely boilerplate." She takes the cooling fax from the printer, scanning it. "And it is, as promised."

"What's going *on*, Renee?" Hank asks, as Renee hands him the paperwork. It's all in long-winded legalese. He didn't remember having to slog through this much paperwork when he worked for himself.

"We are being contracted by V.F. and Associates to help them find a missing person. It's a healthy payday for the firm, with a nice chunk of it ear-marked as a bonus for you."

"And I *have* to do this?" Hank manages not to audibly grind his teeth. He *had* been suspicious he'd gotten out too easily.

Renee laughs, "*Nervous?* You don't get *nervous*. Come on, you've found people before, and solved problems way more delicate than *this*. It's a lot of money for the firm, Hank, please? Besides, you'll be fine!"

Hank decides he's too old to find a new job, and Dani wants to redo the kitchen anyway. He grimly signs.

"Where's this hesitation coming from? Keep in mind that the NDA includes me, so nothing specific."

"I should have read that damn thing before I signed it . . ." Hank grumbles, handing back the paperwork. "You know I've been on the job for a while." Renee nods. "Well, I saw something I'd *never* seen before . . . then I saw another. Then . . . another and another."

"Interesting time at V.F. and Associates, then?"

"I said I wasn't a PI anymore. Then they hired the firm."

"Did you even *look* at the bonus you'd be getting?"

"Honestly, I didn't," he admits.

"You are *being appreciated*. You impressed them with your dogged determination, the same thing that impressed us. That's why *we* hired you." Only Renee laughs. "They're willing to pay you what you're worth. Oh, by the way, I was told a box was hand-delivered to your office."

Appreciated?

* * *

Sure enough, a box labeled FRAGILE in big red letters is waiting on his desk. Hank locks the door behind him. Looking at the dirty glass on his desk beside the box, he moves it aside but doesn't clean it. Might need it later. Hank cuts the tape with his jackknife and opens the flaps.

Inside the cardboard box, he finds a small, well-dressed sloth, the creature Scuff was carrying in that sling. Hank's first instinct is to close the lid and mail it back, but the small creature, curled up on a tan cushion, has a smile so serene, Hank almost laughs.

"Hello again, Inspector." He waves slowly with one clawed hand and scratches his head with the other. "How are you this afternoon?"

Hank looks longingly at the dirty glass. "I've had less stressful Mondays."

"As have we." The creature's words are unhurried, considered.

"So you're here to keep tabs on me?" Hank asks.

"I'm here because I want to help. Don't you find good conversations to be so much more *alive* than letters, dead on a page, or worse, a screen?"

* * *

Hank has his notepad out, ready.

"Please state your name and why you are here," he says, finding comfort in the routine.

"My name is Jay. I am here to help you find my friend, Ariel, who has been missing since Friday. I believe he has been abducted, and there is no time to lose. Therefore, I took it upon myself to travel here and help you, because *I* believe you can be trusted."

"Full name: Jay?" Hanks asks, keeping his tone professional.

"My full name is Gaius, but it was difficult to say, so Jay it became. Scuff and I had trouble elocuting precisely before our minds were fully restored. You know . . . the Fitzgeralds liked it so much they named a whole *Gatsby* after me!"

Blowing past that revelation because it's just too weird to contemplate, Hank asks, "And your missing friend is Ariel?"

"Correct," Jay nods. "We're all different, utterly unique, but few can truly fly. He can, as he's mostly megabat, but no one's all anything in my family. His body, for example, also contains the black and white fur of a skunk."

"A bat . . . skunk," Hank dutifully records. "Why is he named after a mermaid?"

"Not after a water creature, Inspector, but one of the air: the spirit in Shakespeare's *The Tempest*. You may find the Beastfolks' names may be unusual, but your Five Fingers names are just as odd if you speak a few ancient languages. For example, did you know 'Andrea' means 'manliness,' from the Greek *andros*?"

So he's a talker. "Beastfolk? Five Fingers?"

The little fellow holds up his hand with its three long, curved claws and gestures with it at Hank's hand. "Almost none of the Beastfolk have five fingers, a conceit of our creator." He shrugs, or gives an expression as close to a shrug as someone lying on their back can achieve. "Most of your kind do."

"Wait. Created? By Doctor Frankenstein, like he made his son?" It's still odd to say the name and not be talking about the book, a movie, or a Halloween costume.

"No, not that doctor. We were more gruesomely assembled by a morally dubious vivisectionist named Moreau who did his work on an island in the South Pacific. I don't remember him, but my understanding is that he hoped to make servants using recombined parts from several living beasts, hence Beastfolk. There was an accident, and he died there slightly before the turn of the 20th century, now ignominiously forgotten by the rest of the world. We endured on his island until Victor rescued us and brought us back here. I am mostly sloth, for example, with minor additions from some other small primates."

"You're over a hundred years old?" Hank marvels.

"You aren't wrong to be surprised, I suppose. At over a hundred, I'm still as spry and as quick as I have ever been, although I will admit that I've *never* been that spry *or* that quick," the strange creature says, lying on his back. In this position, Hank can see the maze of stitches and scars under the patchy fur where they are not covered by his suit vest.

Hank runs his hands through his graying hair, assembling all the new information. "So Dr. Frankenstein's . . . son . . . is even older than the rest of you. Did Victor do something to make you all live so long, or did Dr. Moreau?"

"Victor did. He modified our blood, which expanded and stabilized our minds, which had degenerated into brutal savagery. I'm no biochemist so I couldn't say how. You could ask Victor what he did exactly, although he won't tell you. He's well aware that eternal youth is too valuable a commodity to allow to escape into the free market." The creature scoffs.

"Eternal youth?" Hank leans back in his chair. "You aren't kidding?"

Jay shakes his head and . . . smiles?

"Who else knows about this?"

"I'm not sure if anyone else does know. Will you now carry me off and bleed me dry for a billion dollars?" the creature asks, resting back and straightening his cravat languidly. "I am at your mercy, Five-Fingers." The creature lazes on Hank's desk, somehow looking even more helpless than before.

"Oh, don't be dramatic. I'm no vampire." Hank pauses. "Wait, are vampires real?"

"I *like* being dramatic, and no, no vampires to my knowledge," Jay says before adding, "I knew I was right to trust you!"

"Eternal youth, though . . . damn." Hank sits back, astonished. "Well, now we have one *hell* of a motive for a kidnapping, at least." He takes up his notepad again. "Does Ariel have a schedule? Does he leave every night at that time, or every Friday night, anything like that?"

"He flies most nights. He likes to hang from the wings of the angel at Bethesda Fountain. That was where he said he was headed on Friday. Apparently, there had been men lingering around every evening this week, but he still wanted to go, hoping they'd be gone."

If it was Hank planning the grab, he would have gotten a team to catch something flying around Central Park in the dark. It might look like what Jay was describing.

"I hate to say it, but that could have been a surveillance team," Hank says, hypothetical plans spinning through his head. If it were me, after a week of no good opportunities, I would put the rest of the team around the park, clearly visible, keeping Ariel away from other places he might land, so he had only one place to go, and I'd lay a trap *there*."

"You have hunted men before, haven't you?"

Hank fights off nostalgia. "Less and less these days."

"I think Scuff will like you, once he gives you a chance. He can really be quite gentle. He's a hugger!" Jay offers. "But he does take 'safety' very seriously. Why, a little girl living in our building recently got snatched right off the street! While not part of a landlord's traditional duties, Scuff took it upon himself to track down the kidnappers and bring her home. The little girl couldn't say who saved her. The kidnappers had drugged her to keep her quiet."

"Scuff got the kid back . . ." Hank records dutifully, but then he stops writing. "Wait . . . your 'gentle hugger' . . . did he . . ."

"Make the news? The deaths of the kidnappers did, but he's far too quick and knows the tunnels under the city far too well to be caught by men in *cars*." Jay laughs. Or at least, Hank assumes the sound is laughing.

"Scuff *killed* people. What's funny?"

"Need we weep for kidnappers? They are hardly the high-water mark of human achievement."

"Well . . . no, but . . . Jay, he didn't just kill them. I saw the pictures the cops took. He *smashed* them. People are asking questions, like 'who's strong enough to swing a man by the ankles into the ground that hard?' Cops all over the city are looking for him!"

Jay shrugs diffidently.

Hank returns to the notepad, hoping that the rhythm of the interview and the moving pen will force away unwanted memories of the crime scene pictures Renee had sent. "Would Ariel have landed at Bethesda Fountain only if there was nobody around?"

"He probably would have flown around enjoying the night

until the square was empty," Jay says.

"But he would have known if people were there no matter how dark it got, though, right, because he's a bat?" Hank asks.

"He can't echolocate, if that's what you're asking," Jay says. It sounds like he's smirking, but his face doesn't change.

"Skunk ears?"

"No, because he's a *megabat*. Normal ones fly around eating fruit and licking flowers, not catching bugs. Important pollinators, some of them, but they don't echolocate. Ariel's diurnal, though. Mostly, we all are."

Hank leans back slightly and tries to look up the definition of 'diurnal' on his phone without Jay noticing.

"Diurnal: active in the day," Jay explains.

Putting down his phone guiltily, Hank says, "Wasn't Ariel flying at night?"

"Sure, but this town is never *that* dark, no matter the time."

"Which is how I saw him, how someone might have stalked him."

"We could go to the park and look for clues." Jay hooks his claws into the cushion still in the box, lifts it up and offers it to Hank. It's the tan baby sling that Scuff had been wearing earlier. It smells floral. "We washed it, as an olive branch." Jay's perpetually sad smile is as unreadable as Scuff's perpetually suspicious glare.

"Maybe later." Hank closes the notebook. "If someone *was* waiting for him at Bethesda Fountain on Friday, we don't have any time to lose. If the kidnappers were in the park all week, tourists have taken plenty of pictures of them. We need to find the pictures."

* * *

With his guest lying on the desk again, Hank brings up some questionably legal social media scouring software. He sets it looking for pictures with geo-tags in Central Park and leaves it to do its work.

"If he was taken by a surveillance team, we'll have pictures of them soon." Hank leans back in his expensive office chair.

"So sure?" Jay twists his head to look up at him sideways.

"Tourists are snapping pictures of that fountain all the time. I'm betting dozens of pictures of those guys have been posted somewhere by now. If anyone put anything on social media anywhere, we'll find them," Hank assures him.

"So much for pavement pounding gumshoes . . ." Jay laments.

"It's a new age, and it's getting newer all the time. Pretty soon, there won't be any more gumshoes, just keyboard jockeys sifting through camera footage and selfies."

In the morose silence, Jay turns his head, looking over the decor of the office: its expensive furniture, its single picture of Hank and Dani on their honeymoon in front of the Sydney Opera House.

"Do you have any children, Investigator?"

"Nah, Dani and I met too late in life. She has one of those big Italian families that's plenty for us both, though they had hoped we might try." Hank sighs, wishing the computer would hurry up. "I don't have much family of my own— just in-laws, and lots of those. They could have made great PIs, though. There are more than a few dedicated eavesdroppers in that group, and plenty of them know what their neighbors fight about."

"They sound like they are all very alert to their surroundings and attentive to details. They must have the souls of poets…!"

"If that's all it took, then they'd be a literary dynasty. My mother in-law remembers every time we've come to her house wearing anything she gifted us, plus where she bought it and if it was on sale. If only she didn't only use those skills to guilt-trip us into wearing all her weird gifts."

"She sounds incredible."

"After meeting *your* family and searching for people who might have kidnapped a skunk-bat named Ariel to steal the secret of *eternal youth,* I'm not sure if anything else counts as 'incredible.'"

"Oh no, jaded already?" Jay sighs. "I regret that. There's nothing that pollutes a poet's soul faster than the magnificent becoming mundane, the exceptional becoming the norm. You begin to overlook the details, and the iridescence of reality begins to go unnoticed-"

The program beeps its completion.

"That was very fast," observes Jay, scratching slowly. "I knew I made the right choice, coming to you for assistance."

Hank grunts as he sorts though the pictures for all the ones just of Bethesda Fountain on Friday. He finds a long string of selfies with a pair of smiling women.

"There was some kind of construction last week," Hank says, scrolling through the pictures, "with cones and tape and everything, even though I'm not seeing a single picture of them doing any work. These are your guys." Hank points at the screen. In the background, three men are standing around an oversized tube that's definitely not a telescope, although it's intended to look like one to a casual passerby, mounted on a surveying tripod. Hank would have wanted a big taser or net gun or something to snare Ariel once he came to rest. Maybe that's what it really is. All of them are wearing nondescript gray coveralls.

"Incredible!" Jay says, turning over and crawling closer to the screen.

As they inspect the photos, Jay points with a claw at one fellow. "That guy in the back is the most important. He's wearing the sharpest suit."

"Suit? They're all wearing exactly the same thing."

"Not exactly. Look, his collar is sticking out a little here in this picture. The others have normal clothes underneath, but *he's* wearing a suit under his coveralls."

Hank zooms in on the man and sees something else he'd missed: the brim of a familiar strange white hat tucked under his arm. "I've seen that guy! Or at least, I know I saw that hat the night Ariel went missing. I bumped into him on the street in front of your place Friday night, right after Ariel left! He swore at me in German."

"E-mail these to Victor," Jay concludes. "This was no accident. We should walk back." The small creature eagerly crawls back across the table and into the baby sling, getting comfortable, smoothing out his suit vest, and contentedly straightening his tie.

Hank, with no safer way to get the creature home, awkwardly wraps the sling around himself with the creature already hidden inside. Hank asks, "This is much easier if you let me put it on *first*, isn't it?"

* * *

Victor, oddly solemn, gestures for Hank to sit down opposite him across room 421's massive desk before sitting himself and lacing his fingers on its upholstered surface. "Could you explain where you found the images you sent me, please?" Scuff looms in the corner. Jay hangs on the parrot stand.

"The pictures were taken at Bethesda Fountain. We believe those are some of the men involved in your friend's disappearance."

"I . . ." Victor shifts uncomfortably in his seat, "recognize one of the men."

"The guy with the weird white hat?" Hank ventures. "I think he could be German. Does that mean anything to you?"

"German . . . Yes, I'm afraid it does." Victor nods. "I'd *presumed* the man I knew had died naturally long ago. Apparently not." Victor opens the bottom drawer of a cabinet behind him, removing the leftmost leather-bound journal from a row. Leafing through it, Victor turns the book around for Hank to see. "Would you agree this is the same man, Inspector?"

Hank checks the pencil-drawn portrait of a young man who, after a few decades, would resemble the man with the white hat. Victor's neat handwriting fills the margins. The writing is in German, but the portrait is clearly dated 1878.

"That's him," Hank agrees. "If he was a young man when you knew him in 1878, he should be dead. Who is he? I can't read German."

Victor translates:

"'*December, 1878. Emil Müller: student at the University of Ingolstadt. I employed him to recover my father's notes and equipment, which the University collected and sealed away after my creation in the hope that their connection to my story would be forgotten. I paid him extra to ensure his silence and relieve him of his terrible poverty. He wanted to explore my father's work with me, but I refused him. Nevertheless, I hope and expect his career in science to be fruitful.*'"

"Father, how did he find us?" Scuff asks.

Victor shrugs. "I haven't the first idea, but I'm more interested in how he has *lived* so long. It now seems likely that he copied something from my father's notes before passing them along to me. My father's process for brewing the ichor he used to create me was quite advanced, but it was only after exploring the journals of Moreau as well that I realized both doctors had been inadvertently working on similar projects— trains approaching the same station from opposite directions, you could say. After studying the research of both doctors, I bridged their work and synthesized a new compound which still sustains us today. It seems that even with a partial solution, life can be prolonged for centuries, but from his appearance it is clear that my poor old friend has not perfected it, even now. He may be suffering side effects that forced him to act." Victor shrugs. "Nevertheless, his reappearance is too great a coincidence. We must assume that Emil Müller has captured Ariel to help further his research."

"It's still so strange to think it's all real," Hank muses, before realizing that might have been quite rude. He begins to apologize, but Victor raises a hand to stop him.

"No need for that, Inspector. You have performed laudably, and you are taking the revelation of our existence far better than accidental guests past. Emil Müller is out there with Ariel, and we need to find them. To gain the maximum value from this capture, he would need a significant laboratory, with both space and privacy. Abandoned warehouse perhaps, certainly in a neighborhood with light foot traffic. Go, Scuff, find our friend."

Scuff nods and heads for the door.

"Sorry, did I miss something?" Hank asks, standing. "Are you planning to look in every warehouse in New York City?"

Scuff smiles. "I will find them now that I know what, and who, to look for."

"Wait, wait, wait." Hank waves his hands in protest. "We need a *plan*!"

Scuff halts and puts his hands on Hank's shoulders, more tenderly than Hank had imagined possible. The swift change in Scuff's normally abrasive disposition makes Hank nervous. "You have done us a great service already. You *could* leave," Scuff says quietly, "but if you choose to stay and help us find Ariel, I would accept your experience and aid."

"There are still too many unanswered questions to quit now. I'm still in."

"Thank you." Scuff gives his shoulders a slight squeeze before addressing the room. "We will report back if the mole-people cannot help us."

While not sure what help 'mole-people' would be, Hank is shepherded into a side room where a wall panel is removed, revealing a dark hallway.

"Oh right . . . This place was a speakeasy!" Hank recalls from his research.

Scuff snorts. "Step lightly. We don't want any exterminators poking around, looking for rats."

It's no express route, but it does emerge at the basement level. Slipping out from behind a furnace, Scuff offers a hand, which Hank takes, four-fingered hand grasping five-fingered hand.

"The mole people . . . Moreau made them, too? Out of what?" Hank realizes his mouth has run ahead of his judgment. "Is . . . is that rude to ask?"

"It's not recommended. You wouldn't ask a person for their

medical history, would you? Well, you probably have ... It's irrelevant here though, because the mole people are products of your world, not mine. Come. See."

* * *

Scuff leads Hank to a manhole in the foundation and pries it up, revealing a metal ladder. At the bottom, Hank pulls out the little flashlight he keeps in his pocket, an old habit from his PI days, illuminating a long tunnel. Scuff eyes the little gadget. "Good. Flashlights are precious down here."

"Precious to mole-people? Moles are blind. Why would they want flashlights?"

Scuff angles his head down, and Hank imagines a scowl on the perpetually severe face. "I *said* the mole-people were of *your* world, not mine. They have eyes the same as you, except they do not see monsters where none exist."

Hank says nothing as they navigate a maze of tunnels. Scuff seems to know them well enough that he doesn't need Hank's flashlight. As a subway train roars towards their little side tunnel, Scuff stops them and covers Hank's flashlight.

They jump down into the main tunnel and walk along the track. As the sound of the train fades, a new sound of people talking asserts itself. Scuff leads them towards this new sound, down another side tunnel that spills into a sprawling tent city, feebly lit by ancient overhead lights in what was once a subway tunnel. Scuff walks down the track, waving to several smiling people who wave back. They are warmly dressed, tanned from being outside all day, and some jingle with change.

"Oh ... ok, mole-people live in tunnels." Hank steps closer to Scuff, whose countenance brightens as people come out of their

66

tents to greet him. Scuff embraces them all warmly.

They step down some kind of access tunnel where, judging from the trail of wet footprints, the mole-people climb a nearby ladder to access the street level. Scuff greets the comers and goers, conferring with and questioning them. None have any leads on Müller but they promise to spread the word and keep their eyes open.

Hank offers, "Don't just look for places that got filled recently, look for security around places that *appear* empty too. They'll be trying to hide it from passersby and cops."

Scuff laughs as they eye Hank warily, telling them, "I know he looks like he works in a law office, but I vouch that he's on our side. If you find the people who took Ariel, you can have his flashlight!" They still look at Hank suspiciously but cheer and dash off. Scuff shouts his thanks, sighs and leads Hank back to the tent city. Hank unbuttons his collared shirt and carries it, anything to look as little like someone who works in a lawyer's office as possible.

Scuff eyes Hank appreciatively. "Jay said you were once a hunter of men and you volunteered to come when you could have stayed home. Do you miss hunting men?"

"Scuff, are there places the mole-people can't investigate?" Hank asks. Scuff smiles at the dodged question.

"The Ritz wouldn't let my unhoused friends look around, but no one would build a clandestine biological laboratory there. It's unlikely they bothered to hide it from the mole-people. That is why they can find it."

"Why didn't you bring a flashlight down with you if you knew they would want one?"

"They wouldn't have accepted my flashlight. They will be *glad* to take yours."

* * *

It's not even an hour before the shouts of "Scuff! Scuff! We found them!" echo down the tunnel.

It sounds like an army is approaching, but it is only a dozen or so excited teenagers.

One says, "I got chased out of an alley two weeks ago by a bunch of private security in Spanish Harlem, but when I went back last week to see if it was safe, there were dudes— angry ones with guns— guarding a warehouse that had been empty. That's them, right?"

Scuff gets the specific address and smiles at Hank as the crowd moves further down the tunnel, taking turns playing with Hank's flashlight. "We'll soon have Ariel back. Thank you for helping us find Müller, but getting Ariel back will mean real danger." Scuff rolls his neck, loosening his shoulders.

"Scuff, I'm not going to help you kill people. Jay told me that you got that girl back, but-"

"Do you know what those men you mourn had been *doing*?" Scuff snorts sourly.

"You hunted them down, Scuff. You aren't a judge. Just because they weren't exactly choirboys-"

Scuff's nostrils flare. "Laws and courts are insufficient here, we must protect each other. You can't really believe every life is sacred, even the bad ones." Scuff stomps, his bare, leathery foot thudding on the concrete.

"Scuff, I work for a law firm. I *know* the law is far from perfect, but that doesn't mean we can ignore it entirely. You can't just kill random security guards."

"I won't kill *random* security guards. I will kill very *specific* security guards."

When Hank seems unimpressed, Scuff rubs his face in thought. "I can offer this: anyone that does not put themselves directly between me and my friend, I will spare if I can. If we called the police, it would put the family in even graver danger, and that I cannot do . . . even for you." Scuff squints without turning his head, the bar pupil twisting in its socket to eye Hank instead. "If you can't accept me for what I am, I'm sorry, but you'll stay here."

"I'm not here to sit on the bench, Scuff. I'm coming. This isn't a one-man kind of operation."

"You agree, then: this is a *two*-man kind of operation." Scuff grins.

"It'll have to be," Hank says, smiling back. "This isn't really Jay's scene, is it?"

Scuff laughs. "No, and Victor doesn't fit well in tunnels." He leads them through a labyrinth of empty tunnels to a small side room with an old safe, which he opens carefully. He removes an old pistol, straight out of a WWII movie, its brushed steel dull in the dim light, its magwell empty.

"I can't be watching you to keep you safe. If I am going to be holding back, then you'll have to be armed. Please, meet me in the middle. I won't lose any more friends this week."

"Scuff, I don't do that anymore," Hank says, touched but still not excited to hold a firearm again.

Scuff offers it along with two full magazines. "It'll keep you safe when I can't . . . *if* you can shoot straight. Please, Hank."

"Just because I *can* shoot, doesn't mean I'll have to." Hank reluctantly accepts them, loading the gun and putting the spare magazine in his jacket pocket. "We'll sneak in, get Ariel, and sneak out."

Scuff shrugs. "Hoping costs nothing."

"As a last resort *only*," Hank insists, loading the gun grimly. "Dani would kill me if I died."

* * *

After two hours of hiking through a confusion of tunnels, Scuff announces they have arrived under Spanish Harlem. Scuff points to a ladder that leads up to a hole in the ceiling topped with a manhole cover.

Hank climbs up first, and moves the metal plate as quietly as he can. Hank waves down to Scuff and pulls himself up onto the street and takes cover behind a nearby electrical box.

Only one other person is on the otherwise deserted sidewalk. Hank, after a quick peek around his scant protection, slips into an alley. Scuff follows swiftly and silently when Hank gives him the all clear to dash across the sidewalk. Through a pile of garbage Hank gets a better look at the security guy.

Built like a refrigerator

This time of night, the rest of the block is deserted

He's standing like he's just hanging out as he looks up and down the street

He's trying to look like a relaxed bar doorman, not private security

Doesn't look tired, doesn't look bored

Verdict: A real professional, probably not cheap.

"I'll go in first, get everyone's attention" Scuff says, "You follow. Find Ariel, and get out."

"Great plan, except we aren't *sure* this is the right building."

"I'm sure."

"Let me check it out first, at least. I'll just walk by, do a little recon, and be right back."

Not waiting for an argument, Hank tucks the pistol in his pocket, stuffs his hand in after it, hiding the shape, and strolls easily out of the alley towards the guard.

"Hey, where'd you come from?" the guard challenges.

"My mothah. Got any othah stupid questions?" Hank puts on a thick Bostonian accent.

"Yeah," the guard says, standing in his way, "where do you think you're going this late?

"To go spend the night with *your* mothah," Hank says belligerently.

"Then you're headed the wrong way. She lives back the way you came, so that's where you should be headed." He isn't being goaded into anger, merely scowling and pointing for Hank to return as he came. Hank tries to push past him, but the guy isn't having it. He doesn't stop Hank getting a pretty good whiff of disinfectant and clinical cleanliness coming out of an exhaust fan in the wall that just *has* to be what an improvised biolab smells like.

"Yep, this is the place," Hank calls loudly, dropping the accent.

Scuff explodes out of the alley, charging the sentry. His eyes go wide even as he draws a handgun from behind his back. Not quickly enough.

Scuff launches himself into a head-first dive, smashing his horned brow into the man's chest. The man crumples and curls into a fetal position. He doesn't look good, but he might still be alive.

This is what Scuff must consider 'restraint.'

"Scuff, look! There are little cameras in the doorway!" Hank shouts, caution abandoned. "They know we're here!"

Scuff wastes no time and throws himself at the door, just as he had the man, to similar destructive effect.

Hank pulls the gun. Now that stealth has been lost, he won't have time to hesitate. He takes a quick glance inside, shading his eyes against the bright overhead lights. The sound of several different handguns and maybe a couple shotguns echo off the rafters. Scuff's bellows his rebuttal. The large open space is claustrophobically filled with freestanding drywall slabs making rough cubicles.

Silhouetted in a doorway is a great place to get shot, so Hank dives into the shadow of the nearest wall. He spent his life trying to stay out of a cubicle, but under the current circumstances, it's safer than being out in the open.

As he leans against the drywall, he realizes just how flimsy this new cover is.

"Shit!"

Hank throws himself flat and crawls along the wall as someone with a shotgun blasts three huge chunks out of the wall right where his head had been, leaving behind holes of light and gypsum dust.

Hank crawls another few feet, kneeling low beside a narrow gap in the wall. Hopefully it leads into the interior of the maze of cubicles.

A shotgun barrel pokes around the corner. Hank fires up from the floor through the drywall, and the shotgun clatters to the ground. Before Hank can grab it, someone nearby shoots through the wall at chest height, showering Hank with flakes. Hank pokes his gun around the corner and fires blindly until the slide locks, then, hoping whoever's there has their heads down, dives into an office across the narrow hallway and reloads Scuff's gun. Bullets zip through the cubicle walls as Hank tries to find something solid to hide behind.

"RETREAT TO POSITION FIVE FOR EVAC," a megaphone booms.

Not a German accent. Whoever's in tactical command isn't Müller

Even if he's here somewhere, they don't have time to look

Verdict: A problem for another day

Men shouting to each other is interrupted by a wicked thump that could only be Scuff. Controlled staccato orders are replaced by screams and more gunfire.

Hank cuts through the drywall paper at the back of the roofless room with his pocket knife. He sits down, kicks out a hole and slides into the next cubicle. This one is full of computers, refrigerators, lab benches and other things he doesn't recognise.

Except for one thing he *has* seen before.

A toddler-sized creature, black-furred and white-striped, hangs upside down in a cage as a bat might, but with his wings pinioned beneath an improvised straightjacket.

A tube emerges from his neck. A deep crimson flow fills a row of vials.

"I smell Scuff on you, but I do not know you," the creature observes languidly as Hank rushes to the cage.

"Ariel! We're here to bust you out."

"Oh, good." He sounds tired. His eyes close and open too slowly.

Hank tries to force the cage door open, but it doesn't budge. "Do you know where the key is?"

"No, and alas, not a crowbar in sight," Ariel says.

Hank looks about the counters, knocking things around, as much to make himself feel better by wrecking the lab as looking for anything. No keys, no codes on post-its.

"Sorry," Hank says. "We're down to the last resort. Scoot as far over as you can." Hank puts the muzzle of the gun against the locking mechanism and fires. He has to fire twice more into the lock before he can force the door open.

Hank pulls the tube from the black-and-white-striped fur and puts pressure on the wound. After a quick examination, Hank unbuckles the straightjacket and reaches in to lift Ariel out. "Now keep still, or you'll bleed out." When Ariel opens his wings wide with a grateful sigh, Hank shouts, "Hey!" but finds, after holding Ariel upright and putting his hand back over his neck in an effort to save him from himself, the bleeding has already stopped.

"We're pretty resilient," Ariel slurs, "although the last few days have made me wish I were more prone to passing out."

"Sorry it took us so long, but it's nice to meet you. I'm Hank Fredricks." He takes the outstretched wings and wraps Ariel around his shoulders. It might be awkward for a bat, but carrying him piggyback should be safe as long as Ariel stays conscious.

Ariel puts his black-and-white-striped head on Hank's shoulder and murmurs in his ear, "Is Scuff off making a nuisance of himself?"

"He's the distraction. I'm the rescue party. Damn, I shoulda brought that baby carrier Jay had."

Ariel chuckles. "I smell him on you too. He must have been thrilled to get out."

"He sure was. Now let's go before Scuff tears the building

apart on top of us looking for you."

"I'll call him."

Hank flinches as Ariel lets loose a deafening honk that fills the warehouse.

A triumphant bleating answers back.

"Should we destroy all of this, then?" Hank nods toward the lab equipment. "Oh! Was a German guy here, maybe with a weird white hat?"

"Came and left. As for all of this," he says gesturing at the lab equipment with his muzzle, "I'm sure the data are all backed up, but let's destroy it anyway."

Finding a jug of some kind of solvent marked *DANGER: Highly Flammable*, Hank pours it on all the blood samples he can find. Then, for good measure, he douses the computers and anything else that looks important or valuable before pouring a trail across the hall.

Hank lights it, covering his and Ariel's ears as well as he can with only two hands.

The resultant explosion is very satisfying.

"That felt right. Thank you, Mr. Fredricks." Ariel sounds more alert already.

"I've always wanted to do that!" Hank grins. "Let's go."

"I would love nothing more." Hank reaches up to make sure Ariel is secure on his back and turns to flee.

The sound of the gunshot seems unimportant at first, and the tug at Hank's back is more annoying than painful.

Two steps later, he stumbles and falls forward. Blood pools on the warehouse floor.

"Not much of a rescue," Hank says, pawing at the bullet hole in his abdomen.

Ariel looks down at his own matching wound. "One bullet, two holes."

Hank passes out.

* * *

Ariel nipping at Hank's earlobe wakes him, but before he can groan and move, Ariel hisses, "Be still! Trouble."

Everything is blurry, but Hank is pretty sure that Scuff is standing over them. Someone has a shotgun trained on Scuff's back and is shouting.

Scuff raises his hands.

"Stay still and I'll lead him away," Scuff whispers. "When we're gone, run. I'm only sorry we didn't get more time together. Goodbye, friends."

The gunman shouts for Scuff to move slowly. Hank tries not to breathe as he feels the gunman's eyes pause on the two still bodies and the expanding pool of blood. The guard steps past the fallen forms, always careful to keep his attention on Scuff.

Hank reaches for his fallen gun; he wasn't leaving without his friend, no matter how much it hurt. Metal scrapes loudly on the floor as his weak fingers get ahold of the pistol. The sound turns the gunman's blurry head.

It's all the distraction Scuff needs. Before the guy can blow Hank into halves with the shotgun, Scuff hits him head-first like a blunt-impact torpedo.

"Thank you for saving me," Scuff says, helping Hank to his feet.

"A two-man kind of operation, remember?" Hank says, leaning heavily against a wall. Scuff smiles.

That's clearly a smile. The world is getting <u>clearer</u>
Verdict: Uncertain. What the hell is going on?

Scuff picks up Ariel, wrapping him around his own shoulders before putting an arm under Hank's.

"What happened?" Hank marvels that he can stand at all. "Wasn't I . . .?"

He can't say "dying." He chokes on the thickening smoke and the thought of Dani getting news of his death.

"Looks like Ariel bled into your wound while you were unconscious." Scuff gently places his brow against Hank's. "But adrenaline and shock won't last forever. Let's get you home and looked at, blood-brother."

Scuff sets his arm under Hank's shoulders. He's warm, solid and comforting, and Hank is glad for the help as they escape the burning building. Sirens are getting close.

"You two first," Hank says. Scuff smirks and steps into the manhole, satyr-man and bat-skunk dropping out of sight.

* * *

Hank has a chance to call home and warn Dani about what happened and what she's about to walk into before she arrives at office 421. She is more anxious about his health than about the Beastfolk or Victor, brushing past them to hurry to her husband's bedside.

Hank rests as Victor summarizes the events of the evening: Hank's injury and the accidental transfusion of Beastfolk blood he received.

"With the significant amount of Ariel's blood your husband received, he should soon be fully healed." It's only at this prognosis that Hank can feel Dani's hand relax in his. "If, once you make a full recovery, you were to report feeling decades younger, it would not surprise me."

* * *

Dani barely leaves his bedside for the next week as he recovers. One day, Hank awakens to find Jay on his parrot stand nearby, chatting with Dani like old friends.

After a week, Hank just *has* to get up and move around. He teeters out into the atrium with Scuff under one arm and Dani under the other. Victor invites them into a cozy little room with several large chairs.

"Please," Victor says, gesturing to a sofa from the loveseat that he completely fills. The three gently land on a long couch. "I am very glad to see you on the mend so rapidly, and I'm sorry that I must celebrate your recovery with a request: Emil Müller is still out there and must be found. I do not intend to put this duty entirely on your shoulders, but we would be much more comfortable with someone on the outside who can keep an eye out for him in places we cannot safely go. I would like to offer a job or . . . opportunity. Now that you are part of the family, so to speak, I wanted to ask for *you* to be our man on the outside, someone we can trust who understands us."

"Work for you, for V.F. and Associates?" Hank asks.

"I believe that I'm beginning to understand you better, specifically that you work best when responsible only to your own . . . initiative."

"That's my husband exactly," Dani says, smiling as he nods in agreement. "That's very generous of you, *grazie*."

"Excellent." Victor continues, "I am glad that you seem amenable to being our representative in the larger world, as an office in the building has already been prepared. Jay appointed it. Scuff moved the furniture around and painted it."

"Thank you, blood-brother," Scuff adds, putting his arms around Hank gently and giving him a hug, "since we already put the name of our business on the door."

"The name of our business? What did you write?"

ALL THAT GLITTERS...

Keegan Young

It was later said The Lion searched for the fountain of youth and found instead the fountain of his death. But those are tales added afterwards. While it's true The Lion found his death there, the search was for the glory of the Spanish Empire.

And gold, of course.

* * *

Promises of gold.

They wanted to find adventure, mythical creatures, strange plants, new food, and lasting fame as they discovered all that the

New World had to offer. Also, to spread the word of Spain's greatness and bring God's light to lands dark with pagan beliefs. With all these tales the old shiphands and returning captains beguiled.

But most of all, promises of gold.

They set out for the New World, La Florida, early 1521. Their exploration party numbered nearly 200. Besides the normal party and ship crew, there were artisans, priests, farmers, and many domestic animals and horses. This, with farming equipment and other necessaries, was all carried on two ships.

This would be the Lion's second, and ultimately last, voyage to La Florida and the New World.

The aim was to take possession of land and begin fortifications to further expand and set a foothold in the New World for Spain.

The New World had other plans, it seemed.

* * *

Alonso and Diego were *adelantado,* a vague title of governance for the New World, though they had achieved the title at separate times. Alonso was short and stout, muscular from many years working on ships, and wore his beard full. Diego was a few years his junior, thinner, trimmed his beard, and always wore on his head a morion—an open-faced, metal helmet crested front to back, which he kept keenly polished. It was a point of pride for him. Alonso preferred more practical things, like keeping his spear sharp and clean, his boots tidy and oiled.

Many years they had voyaged with The Lion into these new lands. Alonso was the son of a shiphand. He grew up working on the very ships his father would later set sail on. He recalled the tales his father would tell of far-off lands littered with gold and jewels waiting to be found. Little Alonso had always dreamed of finding those riches for himself and his family.

When Alonso was bestowed with *adelantado,* he was again guaranteed gold and land to govern in the New World–once they had conquered enough lands. Whatever was 'enough lands' for Spain. Now he was getting older, and wanted to be done with all the shipping and exploring. Alonso was ready to finally earn his gold and take care of his family back in Spain.

Diego was the son of a nobleborn family, and while he did in fact do work from time to time, he always found a way to do less while seeming to do more. He was always finding younger and newer people below him in the pecking order and consigning them to his own tasks. "Delegating," he would call it. Diego was also fond of striking poses he imagined heroic enough for his own statue one day. "Perhaps one of gold," he'd say with a wink.

When Diego was grudgingly granted *adelantado,* he was only told he would be mayor of a town somewhere. Diego had the distinction of having saved part of The Lion's family when they fled their home in Puerto Rico, the Caparra settlement. Alonso was one of the few that recalled that Diego had merely saved the family dog, tiny yappy thing that it was. This incident was also when Diego rescued his prized morion from one of The Lion's fallen guards and claimed it as his own. And had worn it ever since.

Alonso had sailed and fought for Spain for many years. He was soul-weary and bone-tired. All he wanted was for the voyaging to stop, to finally settle down with this gold and land he was pledged, to take care of his ailing mother and now-frail father. He was tired of fighting strange peoples on strange lands, toiling on foreign soil under the brutal sun. He just wanted what he had earned already. Where was all this gold and land for him?

Alonso and Diego, they were not exactly friends, but nor were they enemies. More like companions who had worked alongside each other for years. They did squabble, but they also tolerated each other's quirks. Mostly.

Truthfully, it was mostly Alonso tolerating Diego's mannerisms. Diego would voice his complaints of Alonso's character until Alonso changed his behavior or else moved away from him for a time.

Exploration made for strange bedfellows.

They had crossed to Puerto Rico and helped The Lion repel the natives from his new home. The Lion's family barely escaped. Now, after a few other attacks on The Lion's previously claimed lands in La Florida (by either the Tequesta or the Calusa, they were so hard for Alonso to tell apart), he meant to take La Florida for good. For his own, for Christendom, and for Spain.

They had sailed around the southern tip, to the southwestern side of La Florida. Some believed it was a large island, though they'd yet to see its northern face despite many months of voyaging.

They had found a level enough and not too swampy area to set up a base. Work was underway; farmers and soldiers alike cut down trees and tied them together for fortifications. Alonso and Diego, though they had done hard labor many times on such excursions, were now awarded the most honorable task of locating fresh water. Alonso was relieved for the easier workload. Diego took it to heart, swelling his chest, and his head, to new levels of swagger. It was a wonder to Alonso that Diego's head could still fit in that morion.

Natives had been spotted while they were preparing camp. While wary of aggressors from the Calusa, the truth is their exploration would've been sorely hindered without native help. A few of the more vocally versatile had approached the natives, making signs and using speech picked up on previous journeys to La Florida, and asked if they were of the Calusa tribe. The natives shook their heads. After a barter or two, a dialogue opened towards a friendly, mutually beneficial relationship. It was in this way Alonso and Diego gained a native guide. His name was unpronounceable and un-Christian, so he was dubbed John.

They'd found a few streams feeding the many swamps and marshes about. But they needed something more substantial for all the people they'd brought, for the planned colony, and for irrigating the future farms. They conveyed this as much as possible to John, unsure if their intention was lost or not. He merely led them on.

Alonso found himself and Diego trekking further inland with a few of their soldiers. The soldiers accompanying them were fresher, younger, and less experienced. Alonso and Diego were now the veterans here.

Having been on so many voyages with so many other shiphands and soldiers and colonists, all the faces blended together. Alonso could not be bothered to learn names and distinctions anymore. He doubted Diego had ever tried.

So it was that Alonso followed behind the much-inflated Diego—after, of course, John, their guide. Diego ordered the soldiers heedlessly about to check this or that bush for provisions, stopping at certain trees to inspect the bark while saying, "Ah, yes!" as if it meant something. Alonso just rolled his eyes and hiked up his pack. John the Native kept stopping to turn and stare after Diego and his distractions. Alonso was uncertain at what point

Diego became the de facto leader in this quest, but he was too tired to argue or lead himself. Besides, it was a simple enough mission. How badly could Diego bungle it?

After marching since dawn and breaking for a light meal, they came across a river.

"Wow," Diego said. "That is a big river."

It was, as Diego eloquently observed, rather large.

John the Native spoke a few words, some which probably meant river or some such. Alonso grunted as if he understood.

An adventurous gleam in his eye, Diego said, "Let us see how far it goes." The soldiers looked about with widened eyes. John blinked.

Alonso pushed forward saying, "Why do we need to do that? Let's just report back to The Lion, tell him we found him a river that will satisfy our needs. No need to run into a native ambush or accidentally discover some poisonous snakes or ravenous animals." Alonso eyed the thick brush uneasily.

"Who," Diego scoffed, "is the expedition leader here? I forget. Is it you, or me?" He scratched his head, doffing his helmet theatrically.

"You," Alonso moaned, knowing to argue otherwise would stall the task even further. Diego was capable of holding onto the tiniest squabbles until all else had relented. "You are the leader, of this expedition. Look, you have found a river. Perhaps The Lion will let you name it after yourself. But let us retire to camp first."

Diego casually drew his sword and laid it on his shoulder. He glanced about. The soldiers looked away uncomfortably. John the Native began edging away from all of them, eyes bouncing about between the others. "Again," Diego said quietly, a hint of a threat in his voice, "I thought I was the leader here."

Alonso sighed. Since this new La Florida mission had started, Diego had been rather more full of himself than usual. He doubted Diego would actually raise a sword against him; it was mostly bluster for the new underlings. It would probably do no harm to let him continue to play the leader.

"I suppose," amended Alonso, "we could go a bit further . . ."

"Right," Diego said exuberantly, pointing his sword. "As I said, onward!"

* * *

They followed the river for a ways. Diego now mostly led, John the Native following him wordlessly. The soldiers were whispering among themselves. Alonso saw this, though he doubted Diego noticed. They'd heard stories of earlier native encounters. The fortification being built was for their own safety, after all. There were many native tribes, and many hated each other. A native accompanying them was no assurance of protection.

One of the young soldiers spoke up; Juan, his name may have been. "We must remember, as Spain and God have ordained, should we meet any natives-" he glanced at John the Native—"eh, *other* natives, newer ones, we must recite the *Requerimiento*."

John the Native glanced about obliviously.

"Yes, yes," said Diego, "of course." He was clearly less concerned about authorities higher than himself at this moment. Also, he and Alonso had survived enough horrors during their New World explorations to feel weary of the Crown and the Church. The Sovereigns ordered and ordained from the safety of their thrones while their footmen lived the true travails of the world, surviving some but mostly dying on unfamiliar land. Though Alonso began to see after a time that perhaps they were themselves perpetrating some suffering on the natives. He failed to see the necessity of stringing up 13 natives on a gibbet and burning them alive to honor Jesus and his apostles. Alonso and Diego were, to put it lightly, a bit jaded to sacrosanct morals and rigid rules.

This Alonso and Diego shared, though the soldiers had yet to learn. The young excursionists looked at each other, unsure about the older men's lax attitude.

After more walking, Diego became bored with following the river and decided to track a bit off course. This Alonso could have predicted; it was the danger of putting Diego in charge of anything. Fortunately, Alonso was spared the need to speak up.

Another soldier, perhaps named Cristobal, spoke up, "Ah, señor? Maybe we should get back to camp? We stray too far."

With all the authority his seniority could muster, Diego said, "What *pikeman* is questioning me? Is it not your job to follow orders, rather than give them? You are mere fighters, but we are Conquistadors!" He slapped his morion in punctuation.

A third soldier, Lope, glowered with lidded eyes. He gripped his pike tightly.

Alonso spoke quietly, "We are all here under orders of The Lion to discover a river. This, we have done. Now we must report back."

The other soldiers straightened their backs and puffed their chests out in solidarity.

Diego looked at Alonso, then considered the soldiers with a casual look.

A moment passed. John the Native walked into the brush with an unreadable look. Most of what he did was indecipherable to Alonso.

Diego shrugged, looked away. "Ah, perhaps you are right. Exploring gets my blood up. I enjoy it so. Yes, we've gone quite a ways. Time to get back, tell The Lion of my—*our* success."

A visible sigh went through the soldiers. Alonso felt the tension in his shoulders release.

"But first," Diego said, striking further into the brush, "I must piss. A horse could not carry all the piss I have!"

The soldiers made exasperated noises. Alonso chuckled silently.

Many minutes passed. The soldiers shifted restlessly. Alonso whittled at a stick.

A soldier with furrowed brows said, "Where has our native guide gone to?"

Alonso shrugged. "Who knows? That man is a mystery." *Even more so than Diego,* Alonso thought.

Finally, Diego returned, breathless, face flushed. "Come! See what I have found."

The soldiers began to protest, but Diego was already gone, branches swishing in his absence. Knowing the only way to retrieve Diego would be to humor his temporary diversion, Alonso followed. The soldiers conferred angrily amongst themselves, but eventually went as well.

Following a game trail, Diego far ahead, they went further and further downhill into a valley of sorts. Finally, in the shadow of a bluff, they saw Diego standing with John the Native. As Alonso approached, John smiled. It unnerved him.

Diego gestured at John, "Show him what you showed me. Go on!"

Baring many white teeth, John reached over to Diego's ear, tugging on his gold earring. Then, he pointed towards a black maw in the face of the bluff.

"You see!" Diego said, as if it were obvious. Alonso meant to question him, but John and Diego vanished into the darkness. Diego's arm appeared, beckoning. "Come, come. Look! Look what our John has shown me!"

Lope protested, "Señor, we must go back to report on our original mission!" He tried for a commanding voice, but it came off more puling.

Diego's face popped out from a pool of blackness. He replied, "But think of this! When we tell of our discoveries—a river, but also a cave of wonders! Yes?" And he vanished again into the gloom.

Lope cursed. Alonso slowly made his way down.

Cristobal spoke, "Señor, you are his friend; can you not speak with him? Help him see reason?"

Alonso spoke without turning, "Friend? Not quite. Reason? Not in this life."

* * *

Stepping into the cavern entrance was like submerging into inky night. Though initially blinded by the transition from bright sunshine to dimness, Alonso let his eyes adjust a few moments. A tunnel of darkness led to a somewhat lit area, a cave or underground room of some kind. Treading carefully, he made his way forward, hand out for the walls he felt more than saw. Not long after, he heard the soldiers arrive behind him, cursing as they encountered the obscurity.

Moments stretched into boundless time as he felt his way toward a growing light. Alonso finally broke out into a chamber of some kind. Half was rocky cavern and dripping stalactites to his left, half was dank earth and dripping roots to the right. Diego was by the far wall, staring into it, John grinning by his side.

As Alonso picked his way over the rugged floor, hearing the soldiers arrive and marvel at the chamber, something bothered him. He couldn't say what exactly. Perhaps it was that Diego had been standing still for so long; an uncommon event indeed. Or that John the Native was grinning, something he hadn't done before, as he pointed at the wall before Diego.

Stepping up beside them, Alonso looked upon the wall. It had many layers and striations, some luminous, some sparkly, earthy colours and not. But the one which held Diego's attention so avidly was the thick vein of gold running through it all.

"Is she not beautiful? What a find! The Lion will be pleased with my discovery." His eyes were rapturous.

John the Native wouldn't stop grinning. He was also talking nonstop, chattering in that language Alonso could barely catch but a word of for every 20. They'd only known John the Native a short time, but this was the most animated he'd ever been. He was more likable as a silent scout.

Alonso continued to look about, puzzling at the cause of his unease. The soldiers clustered together, inspecting rocks and roots, making their way over to them.

As they clumped up to the wall, Diego finally—briefly—tore his eyes away from his prize to glance at his men. "See? Is this not a worthy find for our Lion? Will he not be glad I decided to explore in this direction?" He said this, fully ignoring John standing right there.

Juan the soldier had disbelief tinged with worry written on

his face, perhaps the same unknown fear that gnawed at Alonso. Juan's voice quavered, "But why—this place? So far in, under the ground?"

Diego again admired the gilt streak and whispered, intimately as if to it alone, "You could say . . . it called to me . . ."

"The Almighty and Eternal God brought you here. For His and Spain's glory," Cristobal said reverently, crossing himself. Juan and Lope followed suit, bowing their heads.

Eyes distant, Diego said, "Certainly . . ."

"Has everyone forgotten that it was the native who brought us here?" Alonso muttered. Then he cleared his throat. "Well, now to return and tell of our find." He began to head towards the exit.

Diego turned around, confused. "Return? Leave it?"

Lope chuckled as he stepped away. "Well, certainly, señor. How else can we tell The Lion of our success for his mission?"

Juan laughed, a too-loud, brittle sound, echoing sharply off the walls. "What? Did you think you could merely sit here and admire the treasure by yourself?"

Diego turned on him with suddenly furious eyes, as if the soldier had spoken blasphemy. "You! Do not get to speak to me in such a way!" Spittle flew from his lips.

Eyes bouncing between the growing conflict, Cristobal said, "We must return with workers to mine it, for the fortune and glory of Mother Spain. Under God!"

Diego ground his teeth, far too much white in his eyes showing as he glared at the other soldiers. Alonso wondered at this sudden state of mind. Friends or not, something was worrying Diego, and only Alonso's experience could perhaps allay him. He calmly put a hand on Diego's shoulder. "What troubles you, my friend?"

Diego shrugged off the hand, turning on him. "Oh? I have come into a large fortune, and now we are friends? To no doubt share in the fame and riches, eh? What timing!"

Alonso backed up, waving his hands slowly for peace, both for Diego and for the soldiers who were actively gripping their weapons to the side. "Diego, my long time companion, you may have all the riches and renown from this glorious find-" However much he would actually be allowed, after first shares went to The Lion and Spain, that was, "I only wish to return to the fort for fresh food and to rest from this journey. You may tell The Lion Himself of your discovery. But we cannot do that unless we actually leave."

Diego's eyes flitted about with some inner turmoil. Finally, he voiced it, "But-but who will guard my treasure?" He gazed longingly at the sparkling vein.

The soldiers looked at each other, perhaps knowing, perhaps perplexed. They were clearly itching to be away from this place, as Alonso was.

An idea hit Alonso, and he spoke quickly. "Diego, can you yourself not guard it? The mighty explorer and discoverer must surely be up to the task, yes?" He turned to the soldiers, "And part of our brave party can hurry back to the fort, report our find, and send for the appropriate workers and tools to excavate it?" Alonso excluded John the Native, for he suddenly didn't trust to let him out of sight. John was to blame for this cavern, and Diego's new disquieting obsession. "You can all find your way back, yes? You were paying attention on our trek?"

Juan looked offended. "Of course we were paying attention!"

Cristobal relaxed his spear. "We can find our way back, señor."

Alonso turned to Diego. "See? Our problems are not as big as first they seemed."

Diego turned worried eyes to him finally, in something of a friendly appeal. "Then, you will stay with me?"

"Stay?" Alonso barely kept the dismay from his voice. "Why would-"

"Why, one may fend off a few momentarily, dear Alonso. But several can rebuke many for quite a while, by that narrow tunnel leading out. Plus, we are the conquistadors; we must protect our prize!"

Lope spoke, "Why must this be protected so, señor?"

Diego turned glinting eyes to the soldiers. "Who knows who would profane this gift!"

The soldiers were stunned into silence.

Panic nearly seized Alonso, but he took a breath and formed a plan. He would have to stay, to at least keep an eye on Diego. He shooed some of the soldiers off, saying to make all haste back to the fort, report the find and request the necessary help. The remaining he told to post up in the cavern here, some near the tunnel's exit, some near the gold-streaked wall.

Alonso called after the exiting soldiers, "And don't forget to tell them Diego was the master-discoverer of the find! He must get full credit!"

Diego seemed not to have heard, for he was again staring at the gleam in the wall, kneading his hands.

* * *

Hours passed that felt like weeks asea.

Alonso hated those endless weeks trawling the waves. Nothing to do besides daily ship upkeep and preparing for or weathering storms. But those calm nights below decks or days without wind when they drifted at the ocean's leisure, those were the worst. Time was suspended until he could fall asleep or find something to occupy his mind. It took him years to find the right tasks to pass the time. Thus, Alonso whittled, hewing any wood pieces he found on their travels. By now, he'd made countless little trinkets and statuettes. All time vanished into those lifeless lumps of wood, which he slowly but deliberately carved into the semblance of life. Animals, trees, faces, figures.

Then he gave them away.

They reminded him too much of the waiting.

Alonso had paced for a bit, then explored the earth and root side of the cavern for a while. He hoped he would get a decent reward for the finding of this cave, the gold. He thought about the things he would buy: his own island, a nice villa, a stable of horses, a beautiful young wife and many children, and he would bring his family in Spain with him. He basked in the glow of these daydreams for a while, but they faded into disquiet. Later, he tried counting the size of the cave with paces, but it curved and angled in such a way as to make this difficult, so he stopped. All this was to help him forget the odd anxiety that plagued the back of his mind. John the Native sitting there beaming at nothing wasn't helping. Alonso tried to ignore Diego, who had taken to telling stories to the soldiers–this he did while still staring at the golden wall. They also tried to ignore him for a time, but with little else to do, they gave in and sat down in a rough circle around him, less than captivated.

Finally, too tired to whittle, Alonso tried to find a comfortable enough place to lie down and nap. The earthier side had fewer small rocks and proved not too uneven. It was also a bit soft. He lay down, adjusting himself until he found a modicum of comfort for his tired bones. Diego could be heard orating. To himself, to the soldiers, to the gold vein, to God (however unlikely); his words droned on throughout the cavern. Usually Alonso could pay him no mind. But not this time, and it annoyed him.

"Please, Diego, could you keep it down?"

Diego quieted down, but the words still carried. At first, Alonso thought it was a retelling of an adventure he and Diego had been on previously, perhaps a romanticized (and heavily exaggerated) version. Then, it seemed to be a fictitious or future telling of this current mission they were on. Diego's voice penetrated Alonso's weary brain . . .

"...So the great and handsome captain ordered his soldier lackeys to pickax the gold-veined wall. But they were clumsy, or perhaps the floor was uneven, and they slipped. One impaled the other, or some such, but one died. Yet what was this? Upon dying, that soldier turned to gold!"

A soldier gasped. "He was cursed?"

Another soldier responded, "No, he transcended. The gold represents God's favor."

Diego interrupted, "Please do not speak; you ruin the telling. Neither of you are correct. Turned to solid gold was this soldier. 'Ah-ha!' their illustrious captain thought. 'Whoever dies in this cave transforms into a golden statue.' Then his smart but not as dashing second-in-command grew fearful and said that they must flee. The captain said, 'No, we must solve the mystery of the golden statues. Why does this happen?' 'No,' the other said, 'we need not know, only run away.' And he sought to force the others to leave. In his fear, he drew his weapon and slew the other soldiers as they tried to defend themselves. Each turned to gold where he fell. The captain tried to subdue his man, but the fear made him wild. They fought madly, a great struggle. Eventually, the captain also killed his man. He, like the others, turned to gold. So when their beloved leader returned to see the find, he found many statues. 'Good work,' he commended his captain, and handsomely rewarded him for all the gold they brought back for their country. But this meant little to the captain, for he had murdered to create that very gold."

There was a stunned silence as the listeners waited for another ending, some form of conclusion. Instead, the silence rang loud, as did their fidgeting.

Finally, a soldier spoke up, "But señor, what does it mean?"

Diego muttered, "What does any of it mean . . ." He was adrift in some thread in his head, as his eyes were no doubt lost in the sparkling wall. It was strange, but from this angle, it almost looked like the gold ore was projecting out of the wall.

John the Native was squatting some distance between the other men and Alonso. At the moment the story ended, he chuckled silently, and, looking at Alonso, seemed to murmur in Spanish just so he could hear, "The protector of the land . . ." Or perhaps Alonso imagined it, already starting to drowse.

As Alonso finally closed his eyes against the unsettling quiet (somehow even worse than Diego's tale-telling), he tried to expel that rotten dread hanging about his mind like the odour of spoiled meat. Perhaps it was fear of confined spaces, he wondered idly. It had never been a problem in his youth, but after years of voyaging, passing time in those dark, dank, cramped holds surrounded by the close shuffling, breathing, and coughing of other men, maybe he had grown this fear. He'd heard it happened to some old ship-hands. This echoey cave with the other soldiers was starting to feel a bit too close.

Time suspended and distorted reality. Alonso wrestled slumber into submission but it only feigned defeat, gaining him fits of restless repose before it squirmed away. Alonso was left chilled from the cool cave air but sweating from unknown worries. He closed his eyes tighter, willing a full serene darkness upon himself that would not come. Finally he placed his hat over his eyes.

Ah, he thought. *Full darkness.*

He was on the verge of true sleep, when it struck him.

He sat up, fully alert, heart pounding in his ears.

He looked around, seeing the details of the cave again, as if in a new light.

In *any* light. How was he seeing this?

"Diego! Diego, what is lighting this cave? How can we see?" He reached for his sword, as if it could fend off the danger of the unknown illumination, worse somehow than the unknown dark.

"Eh?" Diego said dreamily, not turning or moving from his standing vigil. His morion had fallen off his head, or he'd dropped it. But it lay by his feet, inert, forgotten. Alonso felt his chest heave with more distress by the moment. The soldiers had retired to another side of the cave, closer to the entrance, and barely stirred at Alonso's plight.

"The light, Diego? From where comes this light?"

While he could see the cave, the stone walls, the stalactites, the root system, and the dirt walls and ceiling, he couldn't see where the light was coming from. It just was.

Diego, either responding late or responding to his own inner dialogue, said something.

"What was that?" Alonso said, stepping closer to Diego's side of the cave.

"…the light is every light. All light, always. Forever." Diego was rambling. He was suddenly nearer to the treasured wall.

Or had the wall come closer to Diego? Alonso stepped hither, away from rock formations that blocked his full view.

He stopped dead.

Diego was indeed closer. He knelt before the golden wall. Only the golden whatever it was had changed. While before it was a bright striation in the wall, even with its surface, it now appeared to be flowing out of the wall, towards Diego. Alonso had not seen it move, it wasn't moving now, but perhaps it had done this slowly over all the time they'd waited. Alonso couldn't be sure, having tried to ignore it for so long.

"Diego—! What-what is that?"

"It's my beauty! Is she not wondrous?" he cooed. He reached out hands lovingly to caress.

"No, don't–" Alonso said on instinct, stepping forward. To do what, he wasn't sure; he only reacted.

Diego, too, reacted. He was up in a flash, sword drawn. The blade streaked faster than Alonso would've believed, until it was mere inches from his belly.

"'Don't' yourself, Alonso. Thief. You will not have her," Diego snarled, eyes fierce.

Alonso slowly held his hands apart, backed up. "Fear not, friend. I do not want her. *It.* All yours. I only worry for your sake. Please, be at peace."

When Alonso had backed up enough, Diego's eyes went back to the golden projection, hand smoothly putting sword away. He kneeled again before the now-smooth golden thing, which was more prominent than moments ago. But at least he didn't reach to touch it.

Alonso heard a noise coming from the entrance, perhaps many people talking and moving about. Some of the soldiers went to see. Diego, too, heard it and, in a moment, was standing again, sword in hand, prepared to challenge the possible threat. But Diego stayed put while Alonso went to investigate. Diego belatedly murmured, "Yes, why don't you see to that . . ." The remaining soldiers stood around, not knowing what to do.

Alonso slowly noticed John the Native had disappeared; he had not seen the man anywhere since waking.

Alonso made his way to the tunnel and felt his way through and out to the entrance chamber. Then the lovely, lovely outside. The air never tasted so sweet. He inhaled deeply.

To his right, he saw a group of soldiers, some bearing arms stoically, some holding aloft flags. Billowing in the wind, the royal beast roared silently. The Lion himself had come.

He stepped down towards the cave entrance. Though Alonso had seen him many times and had worked for years within arm's reach, it was always on the periphery. Never before had Alonso been this close, been addressed directly by The Lion, or had the man's eyes fall full upon himself. The Lion carried himself and his titles with visible grandeur. Every gesture was potent. Every word carried weight. He radiated grace and dominance, calmness and certainty.

Alonso hated him suddenly and fervently.

The Lion deigned to spare Alonso a look, tightening his gloves. "So, you are Diego? Show us this discovery of yours. Gold, is it?"

"Oh, your apologies, Sir. I am Alonso. My companion, Diego, found the gold. It is in this cave, where he . . . uh, guards it."

The Lion nodded approval. "Vigilant, then. Well, you may lead us."

The Lion's entire guard tried to crowd and protect him as he bent to enter the cave. He stilled them with a look. Quietly, they decided that a few of the closest (and most intimidating) personal guards (only seven), along with an assistant and recorder/scribe, were allowed to follow.

"How did you find this place, Alphonse?"

"Alonso, Sir. We had a native guide-"

The Lion stopped. "Native? What kind? Where are they?"

Alonso waved his hands. "Not a hostile. John, we named him, Sir. He, ah, seems to have gone out for fresh air."

"Oh. Well, if it's just the one. . ." The Lion lost interest and continued inside.

As they negotiated the tunnel, The Lion voiced his annoyance that they were not offered torches.

Alonso tried to explain, "You see, Sir, there is possible trouble within the cave's– interior. It is difficult– well, you can see, but I don't yet know how– It has gotten to Diego's mind, he will not leave the golden wall. There is something wrong with this place . . ." His words aloud were so feeble, they couldn't convey his dismay of the oddly lit cave, that strange, glittering stone, the effect on Diego.

The Lion attempted to understand. "So . . . you say this gold . . . You fear your friend has grown overprotective?"

"I—yes, Sir. I know it sounds strange, but he becomes more and more drawn to it, and nearly came to arms when he thought I might go near it. And somehow, it's different than when we found it–"

"But you're sure it's gold?"

Alonso opened his mouth but was silent a moment as they entered the eerily lit cave. Finally, weakly, he said, "I am not sure, Sir."

The Lion looked back at him, almost with scolding eyes. But then the eyes relaxed, and he patted Alonso's shoulder. "Worry not for your friend. Clearly the jungle–or cave–miasma has gotten to him. We'll see he's taken care of, back in the fort." At the same time, he nodded his guards to precede him. They in turn readied their weapons.

Again, in Alonso, a fiery animosity flared up toward The Lion and his supposed command.

When the party reached the other side of the chamber, Diego was still kneeling, staring at the gold.

It had changed again. As if whenever Alonso wasn't looking or was away, it changed faster. He couldn't tell. All he knew was now it was a recognizable form.

It was a woman's figure.

The gold looked as if it had seeped out onto the ground, with an upright form rising from part of it. It was perfectly shaped: smooth, soft, hard, angled, naked and bountiful. She was nearly standing, with bent knees turned to her right, her lovely torso facing full towards her audience, showing off all its finely-shaped glory. Her arms were before her, as if to add a modicum of modesty, her head crooked away to her left, eyes sleepily closed, mouth inviting.

All were entranced by this sight, though Diego was completely lost. He hadn't even stirred at their approach. Now they stood not ten paces from the form, Diego a mere two paces away. He was still kneeling worshipfully before it, eyes unblinking.

The Lion, of course, was the first to master composure.

He cleared his throat; though the noise was small, it sounded like thunder in the silent cave. "So, Diego. This is your discovery? Some sort of golden *statue*." The Lion briefly turned a berating look at Alonso before turning back. "A wonderful find."

Diego started, leaping up to again draw steel.

Nearly as fast, three guards stepped forward, pikes both guarding The Lion and threatening Diego.

The Lion was unfazed. He coaxed, "Surely, your guard duty is at an end. We are here to claim this as a victory for the Crown and Throne Eternal. For Mother Spain and Father God. Your duty shall be remembered."

Alonso detested him both for his complete composure and his lack of worry at Diego's state.

Diego's eyes, wild and bright, continued to dart about, trying to comprehend the threats piled up against him and that which he guarded.

Alonso wanted to mention how the statue was not originally a statue, but to speak out of turn now seemed crude.

The Lion continued in that calming but powerful voice, "Be at peace, Son of Spain. You may rest now. Your diligence is admirable. But please, put your sword away."

A moment passed. Diego's eye twitched, but otherwise he didn't move.

One of the guards' deep bass voice rumbled, "You son of a dog, point that sword away! Don't insult The Lion so!" He took a warning half-step forward.

Eyes moving non-stop, enough to make Alonso dizzy, Diego's face grew into a rictus grin, one of mounting madness. His breath came quicker and quicker.

Just when Alonso feared someone would be run through, Diego dropped his sword.

The rest of the party sighed in relief.

Then Diego turned and embraced the golden form.

There was shouting, there was noise, more weapons were drawn (Alonso's even, though he didn't recall doing so), and the cave echoed with a resounding hum.

The golden form opened its eyes.

The light doubled, trebled, filling the cave to bursting. Alonso was blinded.

He blinked back tears as the light dimmed to just about tolerable, blurry eyes searching for that horribly beautiful form.

The golden statue looked at them all, through them.

And then, its arms were around Diego.

It was embracing him, crushing Diego to it. Then crushing him *into* it, only not violently. No, he vanished into that perfect form, as if dipping into liquid gold, the statue's skin rippling gently as he vanished from sight.

Alonso leaped forward, but Diego was already gone. All this in an instant. Suddenly, he did not want to be so close to the thing. Its luminous eyes looked at him, looked inside of him. He felt naked to his very soul. He fell back, fighting to be away from that abomination.

The honor guards stepped forward, alarmed at the new threat to their leader, though clearly afraid of something beyond their ken. They shouted, they threatened, they cajoled, pointing pikes, ordering the thing to cease and return the man. They clearly thought it was a person they dealt with, or simply didn't comprehend the danger.

The Lion tried to call for order. His imperious words affected the creature not at all. "Stop!" Then, it was clear he shouted for his own men, "Stop, do not harm it. Leave her be!" His eyes shone with an odd new fervor. It reminded Alonso of Diego's mad look.

A guard stepped forward. Perhaps he meant to do this, perhaps he slipped on the uneven floor, but his poleaxe jutted too close to the golden form. It may have even touched it.

There was a flash of movement, and the polearm was in pieces, as was the guard. He fell into a bloody heap. A long golden blade receded, turned back into the statue's arm.

The Lion again tried to intercede, shouting, "No, leave it be! We must have this prize!"

Two other guards, already incensed, bellowed and stepped forward. Then, a golden arm was through each torso, armor and all. They gaped at the beauteous face, as it calmly regarded the dying men.

More guards spilled forward, ready to attack or defend, though all gaped with disbelief at the fast-growing pile of bodies. Soldiers from their earlier party joined up with the elite guard, forming a ring. The Lion had to wade through them, tugging them, pushing them aside, even swatting a few in the face with a glove.

"No, no more! Cease your actions; that's an order! From the Crown!" When a few soldiers tore their faces away from the golden horror and death to give him questioning looks, The Lion responded, "We must have this . . . *creature,* for Spain. Think of what we could accomplish with such *power* . . ."

One mortally injured soldier gasped, already impaled on a golden pointed arm, coughed blood, then started screaming.

The thing's head cracked and split by way of the mouth, stretching out to inhuman proportions. It screamed back.

The earlier hum rose with it, as did the thing's voice, into higher and higher pitches that Alonso felt more in his body than his ears. The whole party clutched at their heads. The cave rumbled and shook.

Cristobal rallied the frightened rest of the soldiers and honor guard, despite all still being mostly deaf, for a concentrated charge against the golden thing.

The Lion, ears bleeding, hollered silently in defiance, drawing his sword and lunging at the unhearing soldiers. He hacked at a few, Lope, Cristobal, and even his own remaining guard when they still would not relent.

The screaming let up briefly, the golden statue thing staring, assessing if the approaching figure was a threat or not.

The Lion finally got between all the charging soldiers, pushing or cutting them to stop. Their recognition of their leader halted them, bewilderment and betrayal naked on their faces. The Lion tried talking, shouting, explaining why they couldn't harm the statue. It was still a garbled sound through the ringing in their ears.

Alonso pushed forward, his hearing just catching up now to The Lion's speech.

" . . .for Spain's glory. All would bow before us Spaniards, with this marvel on our side!"

Juan spoke up shakily, "But sir! It is not of God! It is evil, of the Fallen!"

"Nonsense! Only peasants such as yourself, with small, narrow vision, who cannot understand . . . It is visionaries like Ourselves, who take hold of that which is unknown, wrestle it into submission, explore, lead, conquer worlds! I, I can do this. I *will* do this!" The Lion looked with frenzied eyes upon the effigy, adoring its violent aura, fresh blood still dripping off its arms. He held up a hand towards it, slowly, inviting . . .

All held their breaths. But instead of killing him, the statue took The Lion's hands. Their gazes met.

The statue's eyes began to change. They became less and less like a statue and more and more like human eyes. Then, something else, something more . . .

The terror that had begun with the sourceless light seized Alonso. He leaped forward as his heart jumped in his chest. Alonso took hold of The Lion and dragged him back from the thing's grasp, from that unnameable danger.

The Lion cried out, "No!" as if he were losing a piece of himself.

The statue mimicked him, eyes and mouth turning down, but its mouth opened jaggedly. The inhuman cry rose again, climbing past human tolerances.

The Lion turned on Alonso, face burning with fury. "How *dare* you!" His sword swung at him. It was all Alonso could do to block the strikes. He was driven back, but it was also away from the statue, which suited Alonso fine.

The Lion's wild swings chopped at Alonso's spear, taking chunks and splinters, whittling it down quicker than Alonso was at his own hobby. Soon, it was barely one piece, and would not stop a single hit more.

Juan shouted, "Alonso!" and tossed him a sword. Alonso threw his crippled spear at The Lion to buy time to grab the sword. Then, he met The Lion in the middle of another swing, and while fighting back, he worked to bring The Lion towards the cave's exit. The remaining guard made way for him. Somehow, Alonso managed to not trip on the floor or rocks.

The Lion realized he had been drawn from his prize. He stopped and turned back towards the shrieking golden statue. "So be it; if I can't have it, none shall!" He raised his sword and charged at it. The statue's glowing eyes locked onto The Lion, its arm jerking back insect-quick for the extending strike.

"No!" Alonso ran forward and tackled The Lion halfway back towards the statue, both falling and tumbling slowly like honey dripping in winter. The golden arm lengthened and sharpened, stabbing through where The Lion's torso had been, piercing his leg instead.

The Lion screamed in pain. The statue screeched at the miss. The remaining soldiers helped Alonso get the injured Lion up and towards the exit. The creature howled louder, then began flowing like water back into the wall. The cave shook as the ceiling began to break and fall. They rushed and stumbled, fell and helped each other up to race outside.

The humming scream continued for a long time as the party raced back with the wounded Lion. It only faded as they made it back to the fort.

They found it under attack by natives. The freshly cut wooden stockades and walls blazed; the fresh resin gave the smoke a sickly sweet smell. The roar of battle, soldiers and farmers trying to fend off natives together, was duller somehow than that unearthly howling from the cave. Alonso and the soldiers carried The Lion through the fight, feeling like they moved at a different pace than the rest, as if they had not yet returned to this other world.

Through all the noise and the movement, Alonso spotted John the Native somewhere amidst the native attack, smirking unnervingly again. He flashed a small piece of gold, knowingly. Then Alonso and the others were fighting through crowds carrying their increasingly heavy burden.

They made for their ships to escape. Few understood this new separate urgency, concerned only about the ongoing attack.

They sailed, none speaking of The Lion's change in the last moments, fighting for the golden statue. It seemed coarse to bring it up when he lay broken and sickly in his cabin. Alonso did not take to whittling during this voyage. Instead, he stared at the waves, the deep, depthless blue-black, until he was sick of it. The water reminded him of the last glimpse of the golden thing flowing back into the cave wall . . .

They made it to the Isle of Havana, where The Lion died of his strange wound. His leg had swollen, his colour had changed to something ghastly, and he murmured incoherently as delirium took him.

Later, it was claimed a poisoned arrow from those cursed Calusa tribes had taken him. Alonso let that tale continue. He saw no reason to say otherwise.

The fountain of youth story made him scoff bitterly upon hearing it years later. But he was bitter at most things those days.

Alonso received recognition for 'saving the Lion,' even though he died later. He also was given credit for defending the would-be colony, even if it failed. Per the fancy scrolled paper he was awarded, he was apparently a hero. He was given pay–not terribly much, but enough. He didn't complain about the lack of actual gold he received.

Alonso found he no longer could stand the sight of it.

The glistening, the miraculous, these were the things of youth and folly. He was drawn not to that which glittered anymore.

HERETIC, ANGEL, GOD

Kyle Thompson

Heretic

An orange glow illuminated the low-hanging clouds in the night sky, as if the fires of the underworld were following Gustav as he trudged away from his village. Despite the distance, he could still smell fouled wood smoke and roasting flesh.

There would be nothing to return to.

He let the thought drift away on the chilly, late spring breeze as he continued up the hillside. One foot in front of the other. There was no time for grief. If the Holy King's soldiers found him, they'd be sure to kill him and add him to the pyre too. They likely were already following his trail. The spring rains had left the ground muddy, not only slowing him down, but leaving a clear path where he'd trod.

Gustav knew his only option was to get out of the valley and up into the hills, where it would be rockier and easier to hide amongst the sparse evergreens which occupied them. The further he went, the denser the forests would become. Another day of pushing forward and they may lose him for good. Then he could mourn his old life, his—no. It wasn't time for those thoughts yet.

He had already been walking much of the day. With nothing but trudging forward to occupy his mind, he found it wandering from prayers to whichever Old Gods might aid him to vivid re-imaginings of the morning as his mind tried to make sense of the world again.

"Reisender, please hear me now. Help me keep my feet. Warm my body. Let my steps not falter in my flight. I swear to you that I will leave my shoes on your roads for you to claim once I am safe."

* * *

Gustav had been returning home, having left when the sun was still below the horizon. It was well-known that hunters should seek the blessings of the Great Stag in the small morning hours, as that was when that primordial force drove the other animals from their dens. He was walking a rough trail through the long grass with two rabbits dangling from his belt and a young doe draped over his broad shoulders. Not his most productive of hunts, but he felt some pride that he felled the deer with a single clean shot of a broad-headed arrow to the heart. There had been no need for a chase.

Tramping back towards home as the sun was just cresting the eastern foothills, he smelled the smoke. It did not strike him as odd at first. Folk would already be up stoking their fires to begin the day's cooking—and to fight off the cold which encroached while

112

they slept. But when he saw greasy clouds of ash like hideous black worms ascending to the heavens, he knew something was wrong. Then he heard the screams.

No. He heard the last of the screams and then, nothing. Stillness. A perfect quiet that belied peace.

As he crept towards his own home, dread turned his guts in a sickening dance. Each house he passed was aflame. Gardens had been trampled and torn up. Not a door remained on its hinges. Crimson stains told of the tragic endings of those who no longer were, but had been. He could already feel the dead behind him, grabbing at his shoulders, hauling him backwards, begging him not to go and see for himself.

And yet, he had to.

His home looked like all the rest—thatched roof still burning, the wattle and daub walls blackened and smoking, cracking and falling in on themselves in the heat. Gustav had longed to go in and search for him, but it was a death trap. Perhaps he'd fled. That thin thread of hope, pulled tight as it was, was the only reason Gustav kept moving.

He pushed on, making his way to the market. A wretched smell was drifting from the middle of the village, meaty and sweet, but sour as well—like a spoiled roast that had been overcooked. He did not want to admit it, but he knew. Of course he knew what he would find.

As Gustav peered through the smoke, tucked behind a small woven fence, he spotted them. A collection of shining angels, silvered armor gleaming in the morning sun and the surrounding flames. The Holy King's soldiery, but clearly not here to protect the tithings expected of all good souls. No. These were avengers, bearing lances and swords, clad not in gentle, flowing robes, but leather and mail.

To one side of the square, Gustav spotted an archangel. Person in form, but with all humanity hidden by full, gleaming plate, reflecting the hell that crackled and popped at the center of the market. The archangel directed the soldiers with deliberate gestures, swords belted and sheathed to their sides. They motioned, and market stalls were broken down to splinters before being added to the fire, ensuring that the cracking bodies frozen in horrible constricting pain would be burned to naught but ash.

Next to the archangel stood a Mouth of the Holy King; a grizzled, middle-aged man, completely clean-shaven with a bear's paw branded on his forehead. The man spoke with both hands held above his head, palms up in supplication and eyes closed so tight that he looked as if he feared they would spring from his head were he to open them. His face red, he was sweating heavily as his timbrous voice rang out and echoed against the hills.

"—heretics must be dealt with as weeds! The Heretic pollutes the fields of the Holy King, laying waste to all, driving all living things in their surrounds to ruin! There is but one solution to the rot nurtured by the Heretic: cleansing flame, that the field might be resown in healthy land and grow rich from the Holy King's hallowed order! He who is obedient and sacrifices in His name is nourished and fed by the Holy King's warmth. He who worships the false gods of the past deserves his fiery wrath—"

At this point, Gustav spotted a few of the Holy King's men coldly tossing the remaining bodies onto the pyre. He watched as body after body, blood still drying on their clothes, was heaved into the flames. He watched, that thread of hope still strained tight but unbroken.

Until it snapped, one end biting into his chest so suddenly that he fell back. He splashed into the muck. A sudden, bursting sob escaped his mouth as his boy—the only joy left living after the prior year's famine—cast up a shower of sparks and smoke as he joined the rest of the village on their journey into memory.

The archangel's head snapped towards the sound. They extended a single, accusing finger, gauntleted in shining steel, at Gustav.

And Gustav ran.

* * *

The Holy King's men kept pace at first, but Gustav knew this land, and their armor and weapons caused them to struggle in the muddy terrain more than he. He lost sight of them not long after leaving the roads behind.

For hours now, he had forced down his sorrow. His rage. But as he grew more and more tired, trudging through the slick, high grass and spring flowers, he felt it begin to pulse through him once more. It made his arms heavy. Despite being lighter than his pursuers, the mud seemed to be increasing its efforts at swallowing him whole.

Gradually, Gustav's pace slowed. He hardly covered a mile in the final hour of the night's blackness. A small crease of sunlight began to mingle with the fading embers of his home, and Gustav knew that he must stop to rest—to decide what was next.

He spotted a small escarpment obscured by brambles. This gentle cradle of earth would hide him while he rested. But his hunter's instincts drove him onward. If he simply walked over and collapsed in this haven, the thicket covering it would do nothing to stop his pursuers from finding him. They would just have to follow the gaping wounds his feet left in the sodden ground. He hurried past until he felt safe backtracking and diverging from his trail, covering it as best he could by crawling carefully through some squat bushes.

Soaking wet, he tucked himself behind the brush and the relative safety of the sloped ground. He hoped the Holy King's men would not spot him. He took solace that he was covered in the filth of his flight, knowing this might only hide him further. But he prayed for the Mother of Thorns to protect him anyhow.

* * *

Gustav awoke from his fitful dreams suddenly. Exhausted. Delirious. He was not sure what had forced him to quit his restless slumber. The stench of a life now gone still lingered in his nostrils. The memory dragged him back to a reality where to stir prematurely could mean death.

He lay there frozen beneath the escarpment, uncertain which direction he would run if he were discovered. He focused on the sounds of mid-morning, trying to separate one noise from another.

A breeze brushed through the rough grass of the hill, gently washing over him. A beetle clicked and tapped along an old root dangling from the earth above. Somewhere nearby, birds picked and pecked along the ground, seeking nourishment amongst the blades given life by the melting snow and spring rain.

Then. Just above him. A footstep. A dull thud near the edge of the curve of earth giving him shelter.

Thud.

Another.

A gentle metallic tinkling song reached his ears as a new

drizzle began to fall.

Surely, they had spotted him. Why were they lingering? Why not plunge a spear into his chest and be done with it? Were they waiting for him to run? Setting up more men around him so there would be nowhere to go?

Perhaps by some miracle, they had not noticed him yet! Should he just lie still? No. He would run. He had to run!

Gustav's limbs felt like lead. He tried desperately to throw his arms under him—to bend his knees and get to his feet. He could not move. It was as if they had piled stones on his arms and legs, pressing him into the dirt. How had they done this while he slept? And why? What had he done to so anger the Holy King?

He stared at the dirt above him, desperately rotating his gaze, trying to catch a glimpse of his pursuers. He had the thought to turn his head and try to see anything other than the thin sliver of gray sky and the mounded dirt under which he'd hidden, but even the muscles in his neck strained against some unseen force, refusing to cooperate.

A sabaton caked in still-drying mud stepped beyond the ledge of the escarpment. Greaves that gleamed a cold silver followed. It was them - the archangel. They stepped over him, and Gustav begged his own eyes to close. They wouldn't.

The second foot followed the first.

Thud. Thud.

The archangel's right foot was inches from Gustav's face. The armored man had nearly stepped on his head. Gustav couldn't draw a breath. He was in a panic. His muscles refused the commands his own mind was screaming to them. He strained and strained, but nothing would move. What power did the archangel hold over him?

The leg by his face lifted and swung around. The archangel was turning. Gustav had been seen, and his own body refused to act. He wanted to shout. To scream. To beg. To plead. To cry and sob and question.

But gods and their servants are beyond question. He knew this. All he could do was barely flex his jaw and let out a repeated, groaning, "Uhhhh ... Uhhhhh ... UHHHHHH!"

Steel scraped and hummed as the archangel bared their blade. Gustav's heart threatened to burst from his chest as the sword slammed down, certain to shatter what remained of the organ. Stale breath finally exploded from his lungs, clouding in the morning chill.

Gustav blinked and, as he did, he realized his arms were moving. They clutched at his chest and found ... nothing. No cold metal. No blood. Just crude leather clothes slick with rain and sweat.

He sat up and saw no living soul around him. No archangel. No soldiery clad in gleaming mail and steel helms. No spears and no swords. Just slick grass, low scrub, and dirt.

Uncertain of what trickery he'd just woken to, Gustav warily reclaimed his feet. He rose to his full height, peering across the landscape for any hint of glinting metal. Seeing none, he darted from his hiding place and continued his flight.

The light rain was already obscuring his path, and he saw no sign of others passing yet. He had not lost his lead.

Cautiously, he jogged away from his old trail, doing his best to find solid ground and not reveal he had doubled back. A mile or so later, Gustav turned to put the valley behind him again, climbing the low hills as quickly as he could in his exhausted state, keeping his focus on the rocky crags he occasionally glimpsed as he topped each rise.

While he marched, he found his mind wandering with him. Try as he might, he could no longer turn his tired brain away from wondering why. Why him? Why had the Holy King examined his people and found them wanting? As each foot followed the other, he felt like a ghost already, haunting the edges of the valley he'd trod his whole life. The only reminder that there was any of him left alive was the ragged breath burning in his lungs.

Burning.

The only way to cleanse the world of the evils of heresy, by order of the Holy King himself.

But what heresy had they wrought, his peaceful village of farmers and hunters, far from the Holy King's worldly city of Himmalin? What had they done to anger this god who seemed to care little for them? His angels came to collect a tribute of harvest after each rebirthing of Mond, just as the Night Watcher's blackening flesh was beginning to crumble and reveal the bright new skin beneath. But the Holy King demanded little else and gave no blessings in return.

A realization struck Gustav as he contemplated the tribute. Mond. God of time, marking the passing of ages each night, as he always had. The Holy King decreed the old ones were false—a lie invented to insist on humanity's obedience to nature. Mond was nothing but a devil, tricking folk into obeying his capricious whims. So said He that was most high, the Holy King.

Had He known Gustav's heart?

The Holy King was as fickle as all of the others. Just another in a long line of gods demanding worship, sacrifice, and tribute to avoid the worst of their retaliations. While his village hid shrines and kept prayers and practices to themselves, especially when the Holy King's angels arrived, perhaps He had known the tributes they continued to pay the others.

Perhaps even now, He'd witnessed Gustav's sinful thoughts as they'd turned to Mond. Did he also know of Gustav's prayer to the Mother of Thorns the night before? What sin had demanded such a penance as that his son and the others had paid? What sin justified that he now drift, a shadow of himself, over the mountains, seeking the sanctuary of anonymity?

Perhaps the Holy King was right. The old ones were devils. But so was He. Every god demanded love and obedience from humanity but did not return it. There was no forgiveness from gods—only death and suffering in repayment for not loving them enough.

For the first time in his life, Gustav found himself wondering if the gods themselves should pay for their sins . . . and who might demand penance from them.

It was this thought that made Gustav stop walking. His feet no longer felt the desire to carry him forward, and he didn't bother asking it from them. If this was his penance for the impossible demands of the Holy King—that he love Him and Him alone in a world of rotten, capricious gods—Gustav refused to pay it. What more could the gods take from him? His love had fallen to the whims of Plága the winter prior. The Holy King had now burned his son to ashes. Killed his neighbors while Gustav communed with the Great Stag to bring them meat to keep them all strong.

He would no longer pay these miserable costs. Let the Holy

King's angels find him and exhaust their fiery wrath upon him.

Penance be damned. He no longer cared to worship at the feet of any of them. Let them come and send him to whatever hells they may—none could be worse than the one they'd made for him here.

Angel

Jeremias had not seen anything like it before. After chasing this heretic for a day and a half, there he stood, unmoving, back to his pursuers. Why had he suddenly stopped running? Why here?

"Caution," he urged the good servants of the Holy King at his side. "We don't know what this heretic is capable of. He may be begging his dark gods for deliverance even now."

They lingered at a distance, watching for a long while, trying to discern the man's intent. But he simply stood, arms at his sides, soaking wet from the spring rains. Jeremias studied the man's hands, but he bore no weapon. The perfect stillness only unnerved him further.

Heretics had fled the Holy King's wrath before. They always ran as far as they could, collapsing in exhaustion days or even weeks later. Then, they met the sting of cleansing silver and the purifying heat of the fire. But never had Jeremias encountered a sinner who seemingly abandoned his flight. He was not asleep, not sprawled on the ground, starving and dehydrated.

No. He just stood. It made the back of Jeremias' neck itch. Something was wrong.

He worried that the man was working some dark magick or

was possessed by some ancient devil. The Holy King had cast all the spirits down, commanding that humanity tame the world. The old gods were liars—nothing but evil spirits who enslaved men to their incomprehensible whims. In their death throes, these devils corrupted folk and made them ignore the light the Holy King brought to the world.

Jeremias knew, though, that He brought order and required no sacrifice but obedience. If it took killing heretics like the man standing before him to be rid of the influence of the primordial spirits of fire and flood, war and famine, then he'd hunt every last one of them until his own body gave out. The old gods defied reason and sowed discord.

This man's village had burned many of their fields at the end of the prior summer and left them fallow for the planting season. Jeremias knew this was a common sacrifice made by those who still believed in Jorda, the Harvest Mother. These backwards folk believed that by leaving their fields bare, they'd be rewarded with more from the Harvest Mother later. Fools.

It didn't matter now, though. This was the last sinner who needed to atone for his continued practice of the old ways. Yet caution seemed prudent here. Jeremias feared that his men could still fall victim to the strange magicks inhabiting this man's soul thanks to his fraternization with unclean spirits. The Holy King warned of such trickery.

Finally, Jeremias held his left palm towards his men, indicating they should stay put and watch from a distance. He pointed to a pair of soldiers with bows who knocked arrows and stood ready to fire.

Jeremias stepped closer to the man standing in the open.

He watched the man for any sign of movement as he cautiously placed his feet to avoid making too much noise. Despite his efforts at stealth, his armor tinkled under the light rain. It gave the impression that one could hear the ringing bells at the great temple, despite it being weeks of marching away. The thought swelled Jeremias' courage as he made his way towards the heretic. He expected the man to turn and unleash some curse at any moment. But that moment never came.

The sinner didn't move. The only sign he lived was his breath misting in the chilly spring air.

A moment's hesitation could spell death, especially as the Holy King's light was beginning to fade. Jeremias readied his blade. The silver-coated steel would seal any dark spirits in the man's body, preventing their escape. He was still baffled and unsettled that the man didn't even tense. It was as if Jeremias wasn't there.

Jeremias aimed for the small of the heretic's back. The wound would not be immediately fatal but would keep him from running any further. It would give them time to quickly stoke a flame upon which to cleanse the wretched man's soul.

The stab was the only time the man gave any indication that he was aware of the world around him. Just as the blow was struck, the heretic's shoulders shot upwards. He let out a pained groan. Then, he fell silent again, sliding face-first into the mud. Blood welled up from the wound and mingled with the rain.

As he rolled the sinner over, Jeremias called to his men, "Build the pyre for this heretic! Quickly!"

The heretic's eyes were already going glassy, but they briefly focused on Jeremias' face. His lips fluttered lightly, and tears rolled from his eyes. The strike had been clean—the man was trapped with his devils now, despite his life-blood pouring from an exit wound just beside his navel. His will could no longer be of any harm to the servants of the Holy King. Jeremias could see the war of the spirits raging in the man's mortal shell as he seized and contorted.

Jeremias knelt by the man, keeping a watchful eye for any witchery, just in case, while his soldiers pulled dry kindling from their packs and gathered what they could to stoke a large enough fire. The sinner's mouth twisted and worked as if he were trying to say something, but whatever prayer he was uttering to whatever old one could not be voiced.

The man touched the wound in his gut as if trying to believe it was really there. His eyes began to close. Jeremias slapped the heretic to keep him focused. He could not be properly cleansed if he died before the pyre.

The heretic's eyes snapped back open and focused on Jeremias' as he jerked forward, his head and knees drawn towards each other by the pain of the wound in his gut. He reached out with a reddened hand, meeting Jeremias' cheek, perhaps returning the slap, but so gently it could have been a lover's caress. His lips trembled as he let out a single, shuttering word, "Gustav." His lips quit working as he settled back, gritted his teeth, and slowed his breathing, eyes still locked on Jeremias'.

Jeremias expected an accusing, hateful glare, but instead was met with something approaching kind indifference. Holding this man's gaze, he pressed his hand firmly into the man's chest and began to pray to the Holy King as his men sparked and nursed the flame nearby.

Normally, it was the task of the Mouth to read the Rites of

Reform while sinners were burned, but Friedrich suffered from the pains of aging and was unable to keep up the pursuit. Now, this task fell to Jeremias—the executioner who prayed his victim's soul would be cleansed of its stains as they were burned alive.

Long minutes passed as the flame was stoked to a raging bonfire, despite the drizzling rain. One of his men brought a spear along, to which they lashed the heretic's wrists and feet. They stretched him out, increasing the flow of blood that poured out of his back and stomach, thinned by the water dripping from his clothes. Two soldiers hoisted the spear and the man from the damp grass. Jeremias stood and solemnly followed, intoning the words to absolve the heretic of his evils.

"Holy King, we send your stray servant into memory. We ask that his sins be forgotten with his mortal body. Cleanse him of darkness and help us to forget the darkness he has spread with his ignorance. Let his spirit find peace in oblivion and new life when your fires have burned away its corruption."

Careful of the flames themselves, the soldiers rammed the spear's tip into the ground at the center of the pyre, the heretic now oriented upside down that his final dark thoughts might fall to the ground with the ash as his cleansed spirit was set free. Others stoked the fire around the man's head.

This was the hardest part of what Jeremias was tasked with. Finishing the prayer, he was left to watch silently, offering his own private thoughts and prayers to the Holy King while the heretic burned. The smell of darkness as it burned away with the sinner's flesh was horrible, but the worst was the screaming. No matter how incapacitated they were, the flames always seemed to give them some semblance of lucidity—an understanding that their time in the Holy King's Kingdom was coming to a premature end, all due to their own actions. They screamed out their devils while their flesh blackened, melted, sizzled and popped.

Jeremias was always grateful when it ended. Rarely could he bring himself to offer further prayers for the heretic's soul. Instead, he could only silently offer thanks to the Holy King that the suffering was over.

* * *

Weeks later, Jeremias and his men had made the long journey back to Himmalin. The soldiers were returning to their families and dispersing throughout the city to seek rest and relaxation. And perhaps any escape they might find to drown out the memories of executing Divine Will.

But Jeremias had one task left to fulfill before he could return home. As a general of the army, he was one of the few worthy to visit the golden throne and lay eyes on the Holy King in all his shining glory.

As the respective Voice and Sword of the Holy King, Friedrich and Jeremias were always to conclude each wrathful pilgrimage by reporting to their Lord. Ever the Mouth, Friedrich took to proselytizing as they made their way through the streets and squares to the Grand Temple.

Jeremias however, was lost in his own thoughts. He longed for Katarina's embrace—her stoic understanding that his absence these long months served a purpose greater than either of them. And his boy. Theo. How he longed for the lad's crooked smile. The way he cackled and squealed with glee when Jeremias made faces for him. He hoped that seeing them both again would cleanse his dreams of the screams and melting faces. Of the old ones and their demands for sacrifices often paid in blood.

Friedrich finally ceased his preaching in favor of muttered prayers when they were allowed through the heavy, iron-banded doors of the marble temple. Penitents adorned in reflective silver armor swung the doors shut behind them. Jeremias tried to cajole his thoughts into order, preparing for his report as they strode through the white halls trimmed in gold. The faint gray veins in the marble reminded him of the smoke from the heretics he'd redeemed. Or at least, he hoped he had redeemed them.

As they were let through the final set of golden doors by the Holy King's mute Eternal Guards, clad themselves head-to-toe in faceless golden armor, Jeremias was once again forced to reckon with his actions.

Sunlight filled the room from a large, round hole in the ceiling, and delicate motes of light danced across the walls and floor, reflecting off of the Holy King's throne. The clean-shaven old man sitting on a gilded throne and clad extravagantly in fine white silks trimmed in silver smiled gently at them as they entered the Divine Chamber.

Despite his understated but luxuriant clothes, the man on the throne before them appeared as nothing more than that: a man. Each time he returned to make a report like this, Jeremias was struck with an uneasiness. As a younger man, he'd believed this was one's normal reaction to being in the presence of a god. No, not a god—*the* God. Until he'd been a general in the Holy King's army and first been allowed into the Divine Chamber, Jeremias had not once seen god nor devil. The first encounter was an epiphany—a delirium of excitement at the privilege of one so powerful manifesting before him.

On that day more than a decade ago, he felt his faith and service rewarded. The Holy King did not appear to just anyone. Only the most devout followers ever laid eyes upon God.

He often found himself wondering what had changed. Why was it that now that he'd seen this man, he found his faith tested just a little bit more with each visit? He should be bursting with faith each time he was allowed to bask in the divine light of this holiest of places. Few received such a blessing. Was it the subtle influence of the old gods—those devils whom the Holy King preached were imposters and liars?

Jeremias had been considering this paradox for years. How was it possible that he could be so blessed to witness such a resplendent figure as the Holy King with his mortal eyes and yet, he found himself filled with such a pervasive doubt? The only conclusion he'd ever reached was that one must have faith for it to be tested.

He knelt before the Holy King. One did not speak to God before being given leave to do so. Waiting for such permission was part of the ritual. Jeremias did the best he could to clear his mind and exude unconditional piety but found it more of a struggle each time he knelt here. As he got older, it was harder on his knees, especially when he'd spent weeks marching not on the paved roads of civilization, but on the uneven trails that led to backwaters where evil so often took root. After only a minute or so, his joints were leaden and he would almost swear he could feel the marble pulsing, even through the leather padding of his poleyns.

The kneeling continued. He held his gaze on the Holy King, watching as his god's eyes patiently, but lovingly, took in His servants. When their eyes met, Jeremias felt the weight of his faith drive him even further into the floor. He did his best to keep his aching back straight and his head slightly bowed, allowing his brow to slightly shield his gaze.

Not once had he actually seen the devils he hunted and cleansed from the souls of others. Their physical absence left some cosmic scale unbalanced in Jeremias' mind. The Holy King sat in front of him, tangible and beyond doubt. But by being so present when the threat He preached refused to show its true face—it dug at some deep part of Jeremias' mind. He was suddenly conscious of an itch at the back of his neck.

He willed the sensation away. It didn't matter. Jeremias' life's path had been charted long before this day. What would he do were he to give in to these doubts? Surely, voicing such things would be an admission of his own guilt—that he sometimes doubted the teachings of the Holy King. He and his family would meet precisely the same end he'd spent nearly his entire life doling out to others. Their souls may be cleansed by the purifying flame of any dark influence, but he could not help but think of all the laughter and smiles he would be stealing from Katarina and Theo. So he kept silent. He played his part.

He prepared to speak as he knelt before his God and waited for the acknowledgment he always received: "Arise, my sons, and tell me of the souls you've saved."

God

Logan listened to his general report in. Truthfully, he cared little for what the man had to say. But one detail mattered—were the thieves that dared defy him aptly punished? The trials of reaching the village, how many in particular were put to the flame, or how many had fled and were chased did not matter. In fact, a part of Logan wished that he could rein in the piety of those most loyal to him in that regard. Survivors helped to spread the news of what happened to those who failed in loving the Holy King fully enough.

But Logan understood the power of belief. It was so easy to hold command over the masses when you gave them enough devils to chase. And give them devils he did.

He had already forgotten the name of the village he'd chosen to be purged. But he was careful to always have a reason that suited him, and a reason he could give the soldiers. The names mattered little. These peasants had failed to deliver their grain taxes the previous harvest. Sending scouts, he'd learned they'd torched their fields. They had burned *his* grain. The arrogance to steal from God. The move was brazen, to be sure, but resistance was best smothered quickly. Destroying the village and leaving its smoldering ruins for others to find was a clear message: The Holy King above all else . . . or else.

When both the priest and the soldier had finished their rambling tale, he nodded sagely, ready to play his part. Reward loyalty meagerly. Punish questions harshly. He had lived long and well off this philosophy.

"Well done, sons. I felt the spirits of those you freed from the shadows of the old ones the minute they entered paradise. Their souls are now at peace. You have done well and ensured that my light can shine all the brighter in this world. We may yet bring peace to all."

Saying this, Logan rose from his throne, keeping the pain

in his knees and back hidden from his face. He stepped forward slowly and touched the foreheads of both men with a light brush of his fingers.

"Worldly service demands worldly blessings," he said, gliding to a small chest resting on an ornate table by the door. He counted out a small collection of coins. The priest required fewer coins than the general. It made instinctual sense to Logan to pay those trained to run his enemies through more than those who held such unflinching faith in his divinity that they would spread his word, gold or not. Too many kings had their heads separated from their bodies after being stingy with their enforcers.

He would recover the coin from this soldier anyhow. The general's account of the punishment had been thorough and he'd done well; however, he'd given himself away. It seems in unflinchingly pursuing all those Logan had deemed heretics, the man had shared some intimate moment with the final villager put to the torch. His general had been coy about what the heretic had said to him, claiming he hadn't understood.

"The heretic was choking on his blood, Holy King. I couldn't make out the word. It sounded like a name, but he was delirious. Probably the demons trapped in him, Holy King, trying one last futile curse," he'd said.

But Logan could see something behind the general's eyes. It could have been doubt or fear or just a general sense of weariness. It didn't matter which it was—none were good to have amongst one's highest commanders. Logan had already decided that he would send guards and a priest to the man's home in the early morning hours to put an end to this man's service. He appreciated the absolute adoration of his younger generals anyhow.

He passed the money to his servants. "Go well and rest. The cleansing can continue tomorrow."

With that, Logan nodded reverently to the men—a touch he'd developed early on to make his servants feel important—and dismissed them with a serene look as he returned to his throne.

When the doors were closed behind them, he leant forward and massaged his knees, followed by each elbow. His joints had begun to bother him over the past few years.

Logan understood fully that his power stemmed from their divine impression of him. He must hide all his mortal flaws. It concerned him more that as he aged, those flaws increased both in number and severity. He'd already had to have multiple doctors burned as heretics after treating his ailments.

Returning to his private chambers through a secret door behind the throne, he found himself puzzling how best to continue hiding his age. He must continue to reflect a divine example of mankind: a perfect specimen of all that was good in the minds of lesser men.

He could only execute so many peasants before he started to run out of those who could properly care for him in the manner to which he'd long become accustomed. It truly was a struggle.

Perhaps he should pass on new scripture for his Mouths to preach. He could explain that the Holy King had chosen now to appear as a wizened man, the better to share more secrets and wisdom with his followers. Or maybe he could spread a rumor that all who bore witness to the Holy King's worldly form viewed him differently, and that the old ones had found a new trick to sow doubt and discord: that of making him appear frail and weak in the eyes of those who did not hold him first in their hearts.

In truth, the options were endless and he did not have to waste much energy on this line of thinking. Most were eager to devour whatever he saw fit to feed them. Those that refused to accept him could simply be burned in the Great Square before the palace. It had been too long since Himmalin had seen a purge all its own. It usually bought peace for a time. Executing a few dozen random peasants from the city was a small price to pay for order. Most were simply satisfied that their god had not found them wanting. Perhaps he'd just kill two birds with one stone and order the old general and his family burnt in the same cleansing. Fewer logistics.

Yes! That was it. Fewer orders were best.

Logan paused by a darkly stained writing desk in his living room. He took up his quill, gently dabbed it into the inkwell, and elegantly wrote the start of the order:

The following individuals residing in Himmalin have shown themselves to be heretics. They are to be removed from their homes, taken to the Great Square, and burned in accordance with My Teachings. They have welcomed devils into their hearts. All who have spoken to them in the last tenday are under similar suspicion and should confess immediately or be cleansed as well.

Archangel

He stopped writing. Damn! What was his name again? Logan knew that the many titles he'd bestowed upon his most ardent followers only furthered his own mystique. He felt they were silly, so had taken to archaic equivalents in his own thoughts. But servants' names were harder to remember than their functions.

"Ah well," he thought. He'd just have the High Priests remind him in the morning. He could ask them to compile a list of others to join the general on the pyre. At the bottom of the parchment in a careful, bolder script, he wrote out:

THE HOLY KING

With that, he left the writing desk and set his mind at ease as he settled himself at the small table in his dining room. Occasionally, he sought companionship for meals, but he'd grown tired of conversing with the High Priests—a slowly dwindling group of also aging friends who had supported his apotheosis. When he was a younger man, he'd sent for men and women from the city to be brought to him to satiate other appetites. Knowing the inevitable fate of his lovers had only increased his desire, at first, but he soon grew tired of smothering them and dropping them into the chute to the charnel pits below his palace. Despite feeling wistful for those days, that particular hunger had begun to fade with age. There was naught but the bones of his past conquests down there now.

As he aged, Logan found increasing solace in being alone. The stories of his generals bored him—once you'd heard one tale of the grim beauty of a village being burned, you'd heard them all. And the Mouths were nothing but a means to an end—men and women who'd been so convinced of his awesome power they could talk of nothing else. He could only endure hearing of his own grandeur for so long, particularly when already keenly aware of it.

The High Priests were the only men who knew and remembered the mortal Logan, but he'd left that version of himself behind long ago. So now, he preferred only his own company, the taste of the fine food that his labors of inspiring the masses afforded him, the calm crackle of a good fire, and the fine library of knowledge he'd amassed.

Logan pulled the book he'd selected closer and began to read the journal of his father. As he read of wars and raids, he pondered how silly his father had been. He took a bite of still steaming roast chicken and smiled once again at his own genius. Why put yourself at risk to steal from others, when a lie can get you everything you could ever want?

LIGHT JUNKIE

Naomi Artemi

"Payment?" the woman asks you with clear distrust.

You open the lid of the black box, just a crack. Brilliant, blinding light leaks out. You close it quickly, and the box dissolves back into the shadows of your hands.

You both wait a moment to savor the luminous residue coating the inside of your eyelids—moonlight in a world of perpetual night.

But the box is quickly reabsorbing the escaped photons.

When the lingering light fades to shimmering black, then smoke black, then mud black, then dull black, then black black, the woman finally acknowledges the receipt of payment.

"One quarter flux." She takes the box to discharge it.

You scratch at your beard in anticipation—a tic you're glad she can't see.

"Here," she finally says. You can feel that her arm has moved by the displacement of the air.

You reach into the black black and follow the warmth of her body heat to her outstretched hand. It is holding a syringe.

But soon, you are holding it. And soon, you are sitting in your favorite dark corner of your favorite dark alley, tucked away from the dark streets full of people using every sense but their eyes to see their way in and out of homes with aesthetically pleasing wall art no one will appreciate again, of unlit grocery stores to select canned goods by the sound of their shaken innards, of labyrinths of office cubicles now used for the kind of work the VP of HR could never have imagined (even while tugging the slug during his scheduled, closed-door, "ideation time").

You uncap the syringe. Feel the veil of air between the needle tip and your open eye. Even though you can't see it, you blink on instinct. Lashes brush past metal, razor-sharp.

You force your eyes open. You stick it in.

* * *

A white waterlily unfolds. A fly, shimmering green, lands on it. The green becomes the sunlight filtering through summer trees. Mint leaves are stirred through a mojito with a silver straw. Sparkles on rippling water. Golden hair as bright as a 10,000 lumen lightbulb before they were all stolen, broken, or burned out.

* * *

The sound of a drum beats your brain back into consciousness. Your head throbs to it. You feel pressed down into the concrete by the weight of the darkness. At some point, your light-hallucinations turned to dreams. You keep your eyes closed. Focus on the filling and emptying of your lungs. Try to remember how your fingers slipped through that golden hair like wind through a North Dakota wheat field. But the memory is forced—like reading a description of a sunset versus viewing it with your own two eyeballs. When you finally give up and open them, there is no difference than if you had left them closed.

If others bother opening their eyes in the black black, you can't know. But you bother. You're not sure whether it's an act of hope or stubbornness. Or masochism.

Every time you get lit, you become even more aware of what you've lost. What the world has lost. But you're past lying to yourself that you'll never do it again. You'd rather be dirty in the light than clean in the dark.

You feel sick, but you can't just stay here, face in the pavement, drool crusting in your beard, stomach tight as a drum.

As you exit the alleyway, you feel the street open up in front of you. The dark is less heavy here, less stale. Apart from the solid object beside you. You know it is there by the way the air has to move around it. How it absorbs the ambient sounds. Even though the streetlamp no longer functions, it has the audacity to still take up space. Self-important piece of— you kick it.

Yup, solid.

You walk. Out of sync with the relentless drumbeat.

Some people prefer to walk in the streets, but most are blocked by car crashes—drivers panicking without traffic lights or streetlamps in the headlight-eating dark dark. Many ended up abandoning their vehicles, blinker lights left flashing until the batteries ran out.

At first, after the sun never rose, everyone flailed around. Knocking over vases, cursing at whacked funny bones and foreheads hit on corners of cabinets. But as the weeks and months of blundering blindness persisted, a heightened awareness arose. And while it took months more for some to stop stretching their arms out in front of them, eventually most settled into a trust of their senses, a knowing without knowing how, of where the sidewalk ended and the lip of the curb rose. Someone looking for an Alicia told you it was the brain learning how to echolocate. Like you're all bats in a cave, and that cave is what used to be your average dot on a map in bum-fuck USA. *Proprioception* was another term you've heard thrown around. Whatever the reason, people stopped tripping. Noses stopped bleeding. Blind faith took on a new and real meaning.

The drumming is getting louder. You are pretty sure it's coming from the church at the center of town; probably think they're guiding lost souls though the darkness to the light of Jesus or some shit, but you've never bothered to investigate. He wouldn't be there.

You're surprised no one has shattered the drummer's hands—drummers' (has to be more than one. Never fucking stops). There've been moments where you might have done it yourself, but the masses seem to like it. Some way to keep time. A beat for every second, double beat on the minute, and so on, and on, and on . . . because apparently, everyone else is afraid of losing track of it. But you don't see the point of keeping track of how long you've existed like . . . this.

Perfume ahead. Floral and soapy. It doesn't quite cover up the smell of unwashed undergarments. The inside of your nose itches. Sneakered feet pass on your left. Stockinged thighs rub against each other. Bracelets clink softly.

You imagine a secretary out on her lunch break "getting her

steps in," heels tucked under her office desk. But the offices have all shut down. Maybe she used to be one. But why anyone these dark days would bother to dress in anything but sweats, you can only guess. Maybe she has nothing else to wear? Maybe it gives her a sense of normalcy? Maybe you don't care.

"Carl," she says as she passes. It was once a question.

"No," you answer, indicating that you are not Carl and also don't know any Carls looking for their lost one. You don't need to ask the name of your lost one because you know that this is not him and no way his scent sensitivity could handle this lady's level of spritz. But out of courtesy, you return the now obligatory greeting. "James?"

"No," she says, power walking away in her cloud of stale perfume. A flutter of disappointment moves through you. But you leave it behind as you too walk on.

The intensifying beat and consequent headache indicate that you're nearing downtown.

You hear the commotion a block away. Must be a couple hundred already congregated there. *Shit.* You slept too long.

The approaching motor drowns out those who, up until this moment, had waited patiently for its arrival but are now shoving and elbowing each other to get in a better position. It *almost* drowns out the sound of the drum.

You arrive outside the grocery store just in time to see two massive lights pull up. Their light doesn't penetrate like normal. But this darkness is not normal. Denser. The delivery truck's headlights search into it like a deep-sea submarine.

The morning after the sun never rose, people were afraid. Most hid in their homes, carelessly using up all of their candles and flashlights, even lighting multiple at once because they were terri-fied of the dark. When they went out, it was with generator-run strobe lights and flashlights with a full pocket of batteries. That was before folks wised up and started to hide their light behind closed curtains or down in windowless basements. Before people were mugged for a keychain flashlight. Before every match had been struck and burned to the finger-singeing end. Before whole houses were set on fire and let blaze to embers.

All the batteries were instantly gone from every store. Those who saw the writing on the wall? Or had they been removed ahead of time? You never saw the point in speculating, though you seemed the only one. In the early days, everybody exchanged life stories with every body they bumped into on the street. *Had the sun gone out? It was cooler, but not dark-side-of-the-moon cold; why not?* They congregated together for rigorous debates in Town Hall. *Why wasn't the electricity working? How were they supposed to hear news without electricity?* Talked themselves in circles. *Why was the darkness so thick? Volcano eruption somewhere? Dust cloud? Government experiment? Some alien weapon?* You went to a couple of them yourself. It was the sort of thing James would have gone to. But while there had been a few other Jameses, none of them had been your lost one.

The second the truck stops, people gather around the head-lights like moths. A fluttering of frantic pale faces and flux boxes gorging on photons, significantly dimming the effectiveness of the bulbs. You'll never get close enough to collect more than a stray photon or two, and you need more than that to refill your box. The one you just emptied took weeks.

Next truck—another will come.

You hear the **click cla-clunk reeeeep kunk** of the trailer doors being opened. They're never locked. Some self-appointed do-gooders begin unloading the floor-to-ceiling boxes of provisions. Other do-gooders stand guard, creating a path from the truck to the store doors—once automatic, now permanently wedged open. You're pretty sure they're only guarding the goods so they can keep all the canned peaches for themselves.

You missed out on the flux, but you stay for your ration. The line moves quickly when no choice is offered. Some peach-stealer hands you a can. You shake it and hear corn sloshing inside. At least it isn't mushrooms.

Where the food is coming from, you've got no clue and far as you know no one else does, either. *Backstock from before? Warehouse full of grow lights still on the electric grid, somehow? Or could it be that not everywhere is as dark as here?* When the trucks first started coming, the crowd called out to the driver. Begged him for answers. Called him a coward for not getting out to help them unload. Once, there was a riot and the cabin door was pried open. That's when they discovered that there was no driver inside. Someone looking for a Raheed told you that self-driving vehicles use infrared cameras so they can "see" in the dark. The headlights were for show.

As you walk away, downing every last drop of sweet corn juice, you hear voices from inside the truck's now emptied cargo space—people who've finally had it with waiting around for answers. Many have left in the truck, packing themselves in nearly as tightly as the stacked boxes of canned goods. They always say they will come back and tell everyone what they discover, but to your knowledge, no one has ever returned.

You stay.

It's not even a question. You know this place. You know where to find the payment and where to take the payment. Wherever it is the trucks go, you don't know that place.

You let your senses "propriocept" you to the business district. Dusky cubicles in dusty offices.

You once had a cubicle here. Can't do data entry with no electricity. Can't do anything else with no skills.

Before the sun never rose, you would have considered sex in the dark to be anonymous. But now, you know your hookup by the way they smell, by the oiliness or roughness of their skin. And you can feel their face to find out features: nose size, hair line, age. Or you could. But you've decided you like to envision everyone who you let fuck you as gym bunny beautiful. Sometimes you even imagine celebrities. Why the fuck not? Henry Cavill railing you from behind. It's hot. But most of the time, you just think of James.

* * *

You run your hands around your hookup's collar. Down his sleeves. Over his chest. He's thin, but not fit. Most are thin these days. Why work out when you have no one to impress and you need to conserve every calorie you can get?

He smells like cedar. His skin is soft and slightly doughy.

As you take his pants off, you feel it sewn into his jeans pocket: the hard, cylindrical shape of a battery.

When you're done, you get dressed first.

"Hey, I think you put on the wrong pants," he says.

But you're already out of there.

* * *

"Tooooooe Beans!" you call out as you approach your front

door. "Toe Beans!"

You can't imagine how an animal could survive in this. Nothing to eat, but each other.

In the early days, the sidewalks crunched with dead leaves. Now, they've been crushed to dust. The insects are as silent as winter. There might be rats living in some dump somewhere, but fuck if you know where garbage goes. You haven't heard a bird in months. Either they all died or flew to where there wasn't perpetual night. Maybe they were just sick of these fucking drums.

"James?" you call out as you enter. You knew there would be no answer, but still, that flutter of disappointment.

Deadbolt. **Click.**

Your reach finds the chairback of what used to be the sit-and-take-off-your-shoes chair, back when you cared about things like getting dirt on the new oriental rug. It is now the barricade-the-door-so-that-I'm-not-murdered-in-my-sleep-for-this-battery chair.

Scraaape. Clunk. You wedge it under the doorknob. Test it.

You turn towards what once was your living room but is now your barely-living room. The darkness here is empty despite the absurd quantity of decorative objects that James artfully assembled around the place. Empty of laughter. Empty of dreams. Empty even of arguments.

You count the steps as you walk upstairs—*one, two, three, four*—not that you need to anymore. Just habit—*eleven, twelve, thirteen*—

In the early days after the sun never rose, you spent most of your time in this house. Counting the steps from the bed to the toilet. From the bathroom to the couch. From the couch to the closet, half of it empty of everything but hangers. Plenty of space to sit on the bare floor and wonder in what other closet James' tragic Carhart hoodies were now hanging.

You told yourself you were waiting to see if the cat would find his way home, but even you knew that was the ass end of a shit excuse. Sure, James had packed most of his clothes and his toiletries and his precious bookmark collection, but he'd said he'd be back for the rest. Separated didn't mean broken.

How perfectly pathetic—to have thought that the dark dark would somehow scare him back to you like a kid afraid of shadow monsters. Like he isn't more afraid of being hurt by you.

Even though you undress without light, you feel exposed. Naked.

Water still runs but it's *ice-cutting-cold,* and you shower as quickly as possible. The body wash has long since been used up but there's still a few drops of dish soap. You allow yourself one.

You shove the battery into the very bottom corner of your pillowcase for peace-of-mind. James' pillow you put over your head. It no longer smells like him. You wish you had paid more attention to how he smelled, but he was so fucking pretty you barely noticed anything else. You still hear the drumming, but at least it's muffled.

When you wake, you don't remember what you dreamed. If you remembered your dreams, maybe you wouldn't need to get lit so often. You have no idea what time it is, either. If you listened to the drums, maybe you would know. But why would you want to know how long you've been alone?

* * *

You wait in the alleyway until the woman arrives. It takes a while, but she always shows.

She inserts your battery into her tester. It glows orange. Almost dead. *Fuck.*

Worth something, but not enough.

* * *

You head back to the office district. Sure to enter a different building. Watch out for the smell of cedar.

No batteries on this hookup. Even better. A flashlight—at first, you thought it was something else hard.

* * *

She tests it, the briefest burst.

You stick the syringe in.

* * *

A silver straw stirs. Sparkles on rippling water. Golden hair. Bright as a 10,000 lumen lightbulb.

* * *

The drums are still beating.

Suuuck plop. You know it's black beans before you pop and peel the can open.

The answer to "James?" is still no.

The water in the shower is still cold.

You imagine Timothée Chalamet this time.

* * *

Golden hair. Bright as a 10,000 lumen lightbulb.

* * *

Today's menu features a cold can of waxy green beans.

Still no James.

Still no hot water.

Still the drumbeat. Maybe if you just *threaten* to break their hands.

You catch a whiff of cedar and decide that today isn't a good day for the business district.

You walk your old neighborhood instead. Past the basement apartment you once fondly called "the spunk bunker." Where you brought James home from that party after you bonded over both being from North Dakota, only a town and a hundred miles of wheat fields over from each other. Back when all your plates were disposable and you didn't know to use fabric softener. You've already searched there, but the nostalgic in you still likes to pass by.

Even though there are no lights in the windows, you know which houses aren't occupied by the silence. Homes of those who left on the truck or who felt safer living communally in the old mall. And if you're not sure, you just test the door — every house has been broken into at this point unless someone inside has barricaded it shut. If it opens, no one's home.

You walk up the garden path and feel dead plants brush past. Someone landscaped this once. What a waste of effort.

Something else brushes your legs. A tail curls around your calf.

"Toe Beans?" you ask stupidly.

The cat meows pitifully in reply—not a meow you know. How this cat is still alive—

"Peter? Erin?" comes a young woman's voice from somewhere further up the path ahead of you.

You're startled by her presence. Cat must have distracted you.

"No," you reply. "James?"

"I know a James."

The flutter in your gut feels like a butterfly trying to beat its way off a spider web. "James Haart?"

"I'm not sure. We can ask him. He's inside."

You have to be careful not to trip over the cat as you follow the sound of the young woman's steps up the path.

Key in lock, and she *scrapes* the door open.

The smell hits you like a bag of cat litter in the stomach, and you almost puke. Cat piss. Old cat food cans. Cat dander. You wretch. Breathe in a cat hair, or few. Gag. Too many cats to count circle your feet.

You're about to turn heel when she says to the room, "James?"

This is the sort of lost cause he'd get caught up in. Saving all the fucking cats in town.

But then, you think how the stench would cause his sinuses to fill, and then he'd get that inner ear thing that caused the vertigo he was always being a drama queen about. No way he could handle—

A gust of rank air rushes towards you. Your head smashes to the side in a bright flash of pain.

The rush of air again. Even though you know what's coming, there's no time to duck.

"Wait!" you yell.

Too late. What feels like a shovel makes contact with your skull again.

"I'm sorry but they're starving! And it's not their fault."

A third blow. You stagger. There's a warmth on the side of your head. You wouldn't be surprised if it's cracked open.

"I have a cat!" you call out.

No blow comes.

You use the opportunity to fumble behind you for the doorknob. "Toe Beans. He'll starve, too, if I don't make it home."

Your palm cups smooth, domed metal . . .

"I'm sorry for Toe Beans, but he's just one cat and there are so many—"

. . . and you fucking *bolt*.

* * *

Your footfalls sync with the drum beat as they pound out your surroundings: Post box. Dead tree. More self-important streetlamps.

Crazy Cat Lady's strides are slightly off-beat as she pursues—probably hoping you'll collapse from the concussion so she can finish you off. They echo off the houses that line the block.

She's calling out to you. What sounds like, "Just one cat!"

You hear the distant rumblings of a motor. Veer towards it. See the glow of moth people. ***Reeeeep kunk cla-clunk.*** Hear the doors close.

"One more!" you shout as you sprint to the truck, stitch in your side.

Reeeeep. For once, you're thankful for whatever do-gooder is on door duty.

You slide in.

Kunk. Cla-clunk. The trailer doors close you safely inside.

The vibrations of the truck reverberate through you. It lurches forward, and you bump into another body. Haven't done that in a while.

"Sorry," you wheeze as you find an unoccupied spot to sit against the trailer wall.

You wipe the sweat from your forehead on the sleeve of your jacket, or could it be blood? You sniff it. Rust. You can only hope the wound isn't too deep.

There are fourteen other bodies in the cargo space with you. You know them by their distinct breath. Breath that smells like lima beans. That smells like Listerine. Breath that is shallow. That is trembling. That is steady and almost meditative. Your own: breath ragged and irregular and tasting a little like cat feces. Such diversity.

What you all had to go through to choose this truck on this day would be quite the story. If you had it in you to care.

"Erin? Oliver?" asks a woman's tearful voice. She sounds middle-aged. No one replies.

"Amy?" asks a younger-sounding man sitting beside the crying woman.

There's a pause. Then it continues around the circle of bodies.

When it's your turn, you think, *There's no point. What would be the chances?* But everyone is waiting for you to ask it, so you do. "James?"

Always that disappointment.

"Todd?"

"Randy?"

"SinJuan?"

"Cathy?"

"Lilly?"

"Um, I'm Lilly," responds a voice. Every single body inhales. It's like all of the oxygen has been sucked out of the cabin. "Brian?"

"Lilly, oh my god! Oh my *God!* I looked for you everywhere! I didn't want to leave, but I thought by now—"

"I looked for you, too! I was on my run. Then all the streetlights went out. I got turned around. I was so lost." Lily starts to sob.

"I *told* you those late-night runs—"

"I know, I know, I'm sorry! I'm so sorry!"

You have to endure a great deal of kissing and slobbering as the truck drives on. Everyone else is silent. Probably imagining the reunions they will never have. Your head is throbbing too much to think about anything else. Feels as if the drums have moved inside your skull. You don't know if it's the blows to the brain or the withdrawal setting in.

After what seems like hours, the emoting calms down.

"Does anyone else have to pee?" asks a timid voice.

"Hold it," says another.

"I don't know if I can anymore."

The trailer smells like a public urinal by the time you start to see the light leaking through the seams in the door. It's subtle. A dull black against the black black, but it's enough to send your travel companions speculating excitedly. *Maybe there's still power. Maybe it's moonlight. Maybe we'll be able to see the stars!*

When the door finally opens, you see light pollution in tiny pockets on the horizon.

"Exit the truck now," says the voice of someone who has repeated this a hundred times before. "Follow my voice now."

Since you were last to enter, you are one of the first to get out.

"Excuse me," you hear someone behind you ask. "Is it night?"

"No," says the voice.

So, the dark dark is here, too. Yes, you feel it. Pressing in on you, as if you've stepped out of the truck into a thick fog.

"Follow my voice. This way now."

Your fellow passengers stick together in a huddled clump. Something familiar. Though, until several hours ago, they had all been strangers. Well, except Lily and Brian.

As instructed, the clump follows. But you've never been a rule follower. And who knows where this bureaucratic drone of a voice wants to take you. Wherever it is, you doubt they have what your unabating headache and itching skin are nagging you for.

So, you slip away. Head toward the distant glow. Probably just another moth flying into a flame.

* * *

All you have to do is follow the stream of light particles to its source. If only there weren't so many more obstacles between you and it. Street vendor stalls, newspaper racks, bus stops, fire hydrants, trash bins, traffic light posts, telephone poles, signs that once gave important information about handicap parking and where there was permit-only parking and where was absolutely NO PARKING and which days were street cleaning days and what would happen to you if you dared park there on a street cleaning day . . .

And more people. The tone of the greeting here is less "Could you please tell me if you are or have heard of a James?" and more "You better tell me where James is or I'll fucking cut you."

You feel like you've been walking for hours. You find a street bench and sit down beside what feels like a wad of blanket and some soggy cardboard. Your feet are begging to breathe, but you don't dare unshoe them should the owner of said wad return. You rest only as long as you need and then get on with it.

Sometimes headlights pass—it seems a number of the streets have been cleared of crashes—but they'll mow down anyone who tries to capture their flux. No walking down the middle of the street here.

The light is getting brighter as you move towards it. You begin to distinguish mud black from the dull black.

You unclip your flux box from your belt where you always keep it in case you pass by a lost photon. Run your thumb across its surface, slick with solar panels.

When you get to the source, there are moth people six deep along the perimeter of a fence, flux boxes lifted high, trying to collect what they can from the beam of light that lured them there. It radiates up from a central skylight—a beacon of wealth—that casts a sooty glow over the surrounding darkness so that you can just make out the form of the massive mansion from which it emanates. The thump of music from behind its blacked-out windows calls to an old desire inside of you.

An armored vehicle appears.

It inches up to the gate, parting people like a plow through a landfill.

You try to squeeze yourself through the press of bodies so that you can get close enough to climb on and ride it inside the fence. Then stop yourself, mid-shove. Wonder why no one closer is trying to do just that? Freeze. They must know something you don't.

You close your eyes to block out the visual distractions. Let the sounds of the crowd echo off your surroundings. That's when you perceive the heavy presence of the towers.

A thousand centipedes creep across your skin.

When you open your eyes and look up, you see the black black silhouette of the guard tower looming.

The gunshot hits your ears, and you look over just in time to see a body slide off the armored vehicle and back into the crowd of trash people.

You will need to be invited in.

* * *

Life in the city takes getting used to. There are more objects to navigate around. People are more aggressive. More suspicious. The lines for the canned goods are longer. The shaken innards always sound like mushrooms. The drugs are more expensive. They're also stronger. More tempting. And you can earn flux by exercising for a light ration. Whole gyms retrofitted. Human-generated power. There's also talk of work just outside the city that earns you more, but you have to hand yourself over to a drone voice to get that gig. No thank you. Besides, your flux box fills faster. Days instead of weeks. But these weeks, you've been using less. Exchanging photons for information. On how to get into that palace of luminescence with its ever-present fluxbeam glow.

It's not easy. Resisting the lure of the needle.

You finally find your ticket in: she likes to show up to the mansion soirees with fresh arm candy. But it's a one-off. Her bodyguard will make sure you stay superglued to her side, and you'd have to be a very special lay for her to take you more than once.

When you finally locate her house (almost a mansion in its own right), the gatekeeper does not seem surprised at what you ask.

Click of a flashlight, and you're blinded. You used to have a face that got you into clubs for free, but you haven't looked in a mirror in a long time. Haven't shaved in a long time, either. You hope the drugs haven't made you look like a meth-head.

You meet the criteria, whatever they may be, and a security guard takes you through a pitch-dark gate straight to a pitch-dark pool house. The help isn't important enough to waste light on, apparently.

"Wash up. Suits are in the closet. You'll find one your size," the guard instructs. "And don't forget to floss."

"Can I shave?" you ask.

"No. She prefers facial hair."

* * *

You've been made to sit up front with the driver and body-guard. There are only two seats. You're practically penetration distance from the bodyguard's lap. And he smells—greasy hair follicles and pomade.

It's surreal to be inside the car as it pushes through the mass of light junkies surrounding the mansion gates. Every pale face is turned toward the headlights, hapless guppies mesmerized by an angler fish's luminescent lure. So many faces that they all blur together into a sea of desperation.

You hear a bang. And another. The sea parts for you. The gates open.

You can't help but feel important.

* * *

You can now feel the thump of the music in your chest. Makes you giddy.

There's not enough ambient fluxbeam glow in the unlit vesti-bule to see your ticket in, but by the air that flows around her you sense someone that doesn't take up much space. Slender. Frail. She smells like linen and lavender. Screwing an old lady; not exactly something on your bucket list.

"Mrs. Witherow," acknowledges the bouncer. "And?"

Click. Another flashlight in the face.

"Guest," she says, hooking her arm around yours. Voice is girlier than expected.

Another *click* and you're dropped back down the mineshaft.

Something is pressed into your hand—pair of sunglasses. You slip them in your jacket pocket. Might as well ask a starving man to portion control.

The hooked arm tugs, and you follow it through a heavy velvet curtain. The clouds part. The long dark tunnel ends. And you step into white.

You hear yourself gasp. The body beside you giggles.

There is movement. Blurry shapes swimming through the milky light. You squint. The shapes move to the rhythm of the music. You realize they must be dancing.

The arm pulls again, and you are led toward Nirvana.

As your eyes adjust, you start to see colors emerge. A figure in cobalt blue, another in lipstick red. Beside you; iridescent lilac. *Color without a needle in the eye!* Silver trays float by carrying cocktails. Liquid amber and grapefruit pink and apple green. The waiters wear gold stripper-skimpy uniforms instead of tuxes. Others entertain on the dance floor. One, lathered in glitter with slicked-back blonde hair . . .

There he is, sparkling like a disco ball, spectacular to behold. Your estranged husband. James.

You blink. Make sure you're not light-hallucinating.

He stops dancing and just stares at you. You wonder if he looks so shocked because he's surprised to see you or if you really look that shit.

He slides through the gyrating bodies until he is standing only an arm's length away.

You want to say how you wandered the streets thinking of no one but him. How sorry you are for not appreciating him before. How you only exist for the drugs that let you relive that day by the lake where the sun shone off his golden hair and you realized you wanted to marry him. But all you say is, "The cat is gone."

"He's here," James says.

"Toe Beans? You took him?"

"I didn't want him to starve."

A slight tug on your elbow—Witherow has turned to speak with someone on her other side. You see her in focus for the first time. Do a double-take. Her hair is styled in a sweeping bob similar to that of the mature woman she's in conversation with, only it's strawberry blonde. She's wearing a full face of make-up but doesn't need it. Lilac ball gown is classy but slightly too big. And too formal for someone her age. Twenty-something? Makes you question how accurate your assumptions were in the business district . . .

"So, you're with the Witherow heiress."

"I didn't know her before today," you answer truthfully.

You can see in his eyes that James doesn't believe you, but even in the dark, you would know. You lost his trust long before any of this.

You notice Agent Pomade—stance wide, hands clasped at his groin—eying you from his proper station several paces behind. Angle your body more in the direction of your ticket's conversation.

James gets the hint. "I have to get back. I'll find you later. You can see Toe Beans if you want."

"I would have fed the cat," you say as he dances away. You've never seen him dance a day in your life, before.

* * *

You keep having to remind yourself that you're not

light- hallucinating the silver platters of hors d'oeuvres and champagne flutes floating through the clusters of bejeweled guests. The arm that remains firmly hooked around yours, models its own extravagant emerald bracelet. Public displays of wealth; weird how this shit still matters here. Diamonds don't even buy batteries out in the dark dark.

But flux does.

You glance down at your box. Already full. *Now who's rich, bitch?*

It's clear Witherow is showing you off. "Just because they don't have light resources, doesn't mean that they're not still human beings." Dragging you from boring old rich lady—"Oh, yes, his life was *abominable* before the Witherow Foundation's new initiative came to his aid,"—to boring old rich lady—"You're too kind, but I credit my parents' philanthropic spirit."

You thought this was a sex thing. Or maybe it is, and this is just the foreplay.

As the evening progresses, you piece together your ticket's backstory: parents on a private jet the morning the sun never rose. Never landed at their destination. (Old lady clothes suddenly make sense; obviously her mother's.) An orphan seeking validation from her parents' peers. Tragic. Would be more tragic if she wasn't exploiting your misfortune to appear superior.

You keep your eye out for James, but the fashionably late crowd have added their jewels to the exhibition. You only catch flashes of the skimpy gold uniforms slipping between the press of guests. No way to tell if any belong to him.

You're on edge. *What if he doesn't come back?* Then you remind yourself that this is the man who once helped the neighbor mulch his entire back yard right after having an anaphylactic attack—EpiPenned himself in the thigh like he was sticking in a fucking roast turkey thermometer—because he had 'said he would.'

* * *

A couple hours later, James brushes past you and whispers, "Bathroom."

* * *

"I hate the beard," he wastes no time telling you.

"And here I thought I was entering my era of hobo chic."

James gives you his 'not amused' face, but you catch a hint of smirk.

He pushes open a granite stall door. On the closed seat is a monogrammed towel. Folded. With a razor placed on top.

Maybe before the sun never rose, you would have been repulsed by having to shave in a toilet. There's a lot you've done in the dark that would have turned your stomach in the light.

When you go to dry your face, you discover, tucked into the towel, one of the golden waiter uniforms. You shed the suit and leave it in the empty stall.

Agent Pomade is still waiting outside the bathroom door where you left him. He lets you pass. You chance a glance back and see him shifting foot to foot. Getting antsy.

The uniform is skintight even though you're mostly bones. You keep checking your bulge to make sure it isn't lopsided or anything. You've gotten so used to playing pocket pool in public that you've forgotten how to be discreet about it.

James slides up next to you and hands you a tray. "Heard of hiding in plain sight?"

* * *

You weave through the crowd. A hand grabs a drink here, sets down an empty glass there. One hand with an emerald bracelet places a drained champagne flute on your tray.

"...starving on the streets before we saved him," your ticket in is telling an older woman with bright white hair that only looks gray in contrast to the surplus of pearls that drip from her every appendage. "I'll have him tell you all about it when he rejoins us. Shortly." She looks toward the bathrooms. Straight past you.

She's trying to hide it, but you can tell she's pissed.

"Every person matters, you know," you hear her boast in feigned modesty as you move away. Far away.

* * *

There is no sunrise, but you sense the party is dwindling into early morning. Finally, James says, "Let's clock out."

They have clocks here.

* * *

You collect the cat from the storage closet where James keeps him while he's working. Find a vacant bedroom and claim it for yourselves—staff get bunks but no privacy.

The room is drenched in drapery. Quilted velvet. Royal blue.

Only one bed, but it's a California King.

* * *

You may never have noticed his smell before but it is immediately familiar to you. Now you can define notes of musk and sweetgrass too.

"Are you wearing cologne?" you ask.

"The soap is scented here. *All* of it."

"But your sinuses..."

"I'm fine, I'm fine." He waves your concern away and goes

back to petting Toe Beans who is stretched out between you and James on the royal blue velvet bedspread. His ginger fur vibrates as he purrs. *Cute little cock-blocker.*

"But have you been dizzy?"

"They have antihistamines here."

"They get you all groggy. And the non-drowsy shit—"

"I'm fine!" Looks you in the eyes. "I promise."

You always found his sincerity to be a little unsettling. So, you look away. Watch your fingertips run through his hair—*wind through wheat*—down his cheek bone, his jawline, his Adam's apple, his collarbone, his biceps . . .

"You've been working out."

"They like us to."

"You hate working out."

He shrugs.

"How'd you get this gig, anyway?"

James plays with the cat's paw, pressing the footpad so the toe beans fan out, then releasing the pressure and watching them snap back together. "I'd rather not talk about that yet, if you don't mind."

You mind.

"How long have you been here, then?" *In this golden fucking light palace, while I've been fumbling through the world like a mouse stuck in a storage closet,* you want to say. But you refrain. You've learned the hard way that if you let your thoughts pour brain to tongue before filtering first, all you'll taste is foot. "If you took the cat, you must have left right after it happened?"

"I assumed you left on the first truck." Is that a hint of apology in his voice?

"Did you even look for me?" you ask as casually as you can.

"I looked. When I went to get Toe Beans."

You don't know what to say to that. He looked. But he didn't wait.

You pick at a button on the quilted bedspread.

You've never been good with awkward silences. "So . . . do you know what the fuck *happened?*"

He laughs.

You laugh.

Toe Beans unslits his eyes to give the humans a dirty look.

Clearly relieved to change the subject, James dives in. "OK, what we know for sure is—" He tells you how there was some sort of military operation during the Cold War called 'Project Needles' where Nixon tried to up America's global military communications game by sending 500 million tiny needles into the ionosphere. "Where electrically charged particles reflect radio waves back to Earth," he explains, knowing that you wouldn't have the faintest idea otherwise.

But you're only half listening. The other half of you is thinking how pretty he still is. It's not like you forgot, but memories are like reflections in a smudgy mirror—your bathroom mirror before you moved in with James and his Windex obsession.

Those pretty lips continue to tell you how the head of some telecommunications conglomerate, apparently inspired by Nixon's unrealized vision, "and hubris," gave himself the authority to launch a new wave of them, only not needles, microscopic satellites, and only not 500 million, but over a *billion*. Surprise, surprise, it had unintended effects. The ionosphere normally only blocks out certain ultraviolet rays, but these "nanolites" (you snort) altered the ionosphere's gases in some way. Now, the electrically charged particles reflect light back into space, effectively blocking out the sunlight. "Thank God certain infrared wavelengths still make it through, otherwise the Earth would have frozen solid. Humanity exterminated for faster streaming of memes!"

It takes you a moment to register that the explanation has reached its end.

James was always the smart one, so you trust that he's sourced the science shit. There's really only one question to be asked: "Who's we?"

"What?"

"You said, what *we* know. Who is 'we'?" you ask again. James was always the smart one; you were always the jealous one.

You can tell by the way he bites his cheek that James wishes he'd chosen his words more carefully. "It's better you don't know."

"Is there someone else?" you ask, not really wanting the answer.

"No, no. It's not that." Now James picks at the velvet-covered button. "I just . . . can't tell you."

"But I'm your husband."

"We're getting divorced."

You can't tell if he's joking. He always did have a dry sense of humor. You decide to pretend he is. "I don't think the government office that issues divorce papers is open for business these days," you respond playfully.

"We're still separated."

He doesn't return your playful tone.

* * *

You can't sleep. The stench of detergent on the comforter

is too strong. The air too dry. Too stale. And James shut off the light—as if to punctuate his point—after telling you to "just drop it already." Opposite side of the California King.

You've pretended to roll over in your sleep twice already, but there's still a queen-sized chasm between you. You flop over once more. Let the back of your hand touch the skin of his shoulder.

But James pretends to be asleep, too.

You sense the black black climbing the walls of the mansion like invasive ivy. Trying to find a crack to worm in through.

When finally you drift off, finally, you dream. Of shadowy back alleyways and mystery cans of produces being shaken down dark isles.

Some time in the night one of you rolls into the other and, "separated" or not, you fall back into old habits.

* * *

It's the next morning. Or so the clock tells you. Toe Beans is kneading your pillow and purring loudly. James' bedside lamp casts a halo behind his head. The more you stare, the more it shimmers.

"So . . . is this all from flux boxes?" you ask him, trying hard not to blink. "Or can't you tell me that, either?" You meant to tease but it came out more bitter. You tense.

James smiles at you; an *oh-you-are-so-clueless-it's-adorable* sort of smile. "These people aren't the type to buy flux by the box."

He's teasing you back. Your shoulders relax some.

"Batteries then? They disappeared from all the stores."

This time he laughs at you out loud. "These also aren't the type to buy batteries in the store. They buy battery *factories*. Some you'll meet here, they were just lucky enough to have a small off-the-grid energy source and became light-rich overnight. But most, they own the nuclear power plants, hydroelectric dams, wind farms, geothermal pumps . . . everything."

Doesn't make any fucking sense.

"Doesn't make sense," you voice. "If there are wind farms and shit, why doesn't the electricity work, then?"

Deadpan, he says, "It does. It's just being siphoned off."

"You're fucking with me."

"I wish I was." It's still so damn sexy when he furrows his brow like that.

"Do you, now?"

After the sun never rose, anytime you craved James you had to scrounge up payment and jab a needle of unknown origin in your eye. Now you can just—

James turns his face away before your lips can touch his. "About last night . . ."

Fuck. Shit. "I knew there was someone else." You catch a whiff of cedar float through your memory. Yes, you're aware you're being a hypocrite, but jealousy doesn't give two shits about logic.

"I told you, it's not that. It's just . . . we broke up—"

"Separated," you correct him.

"—for a reason."

"Does any of that matter now?"

"I don't know," he replies pensively. He looks off to the side at some spot on the plush carpet. There he goes, overthinking again.

"Why help me ditch Witherow, then?"

"Because . . . I know her modus operandi. She never brings a guest more than once. And because I know that once you leave here—unless you can buy your way—you won't make it back in."

"So, you do want me here." *Validate me!* you want to scream.

"I wanted to make sure you were safe." He looks back at you, brow still creased. "You don't look well."

He's not wrong. Still, not nice.

"Thanks." You keep your face stony. "So last night, that was pity sex, was it?"

James sighs. You know he's thinking you're being too reactionary. And maybe you are. But his words sting. Or is that just the bite of withdrawal? You've been using less these last weeks, but less is not none. Now it's none.

"I never stopped looking for you, you know. All the while you were here, playing fuckboy." You feel the resentment blistering its way up your throat. "You cared more about the fucking cat than me."

"If we're getting into all of *this*, I need breakfast first." James gets up and shimmies his absurd gold uniform back on. You look away, already regretting your outburst. "Do you want some?" you hear him ask gently.

Your hunger is louder than your ego. "Long as it's not canned mushrooms."

* * *

You open all the drawers. Look in the closet. Nothing of value. Not back-alley value, anyway.

You're back under the bedspread by the time James returns. He's carrying a plate heaped with continental breakfast staples: croissants and jam, waffles with syrup, scrambled eggs. And coffee. The smell makes you want to cum.

Out there in the dark dark, the daily canned ration was your only option. Some people savored it. You got it over with. It was just fuel. Fuel to get your body where you needed to get it to. Fuel to get done what you needed to get done. A means to an end. And that end was always the tip of a needle.

But *this*—you take a bite of the croissant and let the butterfat coat the roof of your mouth. The sweetness of the raspberry jam rolls over your tongue. Then the tartness smacks you in the back of the jaw. Saliva squirts. You moan.

"Good?" James laughs.

"Mmmhmm," you reply, mouth so full you can barely chew. You cram another bite in.

"You'll make yourself sick! There's plenty more where this came from."

You swallow. Slow down. Savor.

The thing about apologies is it's best to get them over with. Before the hurt festers in the heart you've wounded. "I'm sorry, muffin top," you offer. "You know I get hangry."

"I know." Your husband is nothing if not empathetic.

"Imagine what a bitch I was living off of one can of beans a day!"

His voice is soft. "I can only imagine." His halo shimmers. It's like he's a saint trying to empathize with a sinner on how shitty Hell is.

You can't stop staring at the lamp behind his head. You're seeing sunspots now.

"So, if the electricity works . . . why the flux boxes?"

"So those with more can control those with less," James says cynically.

"Elaborate?"

"Just a way for The Committee to create a new currency." Off your look—"New government made up of the same old corporate lobbyists who ran it before, anyway," he rants. "Entrepreneurial grifters."

"Are they behind the trucks, too?"

"They pretend it's philanthropy."

You think about the huddle of your fellow passengers blindly following that bureaucratic drone of a voice into the unknown.

"What do you mean by, 'they pretend?'"

"Is that the time? Better get ready for my shift," James deflects. "Just gonna hop in the shower real quick."

You roll out of bed to follow.

"Mind making the bed?" he asks before closing the bathroom door on you.

While the shower runs, you throw the comforter over the mess of sheets. Then dress. You're not one to feel immodest, but this fucking uniform . . . You've seen less skimpy outfits at circuit parties.

"What are you doing?" asks James.

He dressed in the bathroom.

"What does it look like?"

"They don't just let anyone work here."

"But if I'm not working, why would they let me stay?"

His lack of answer says it all. You see the shadow of back alleyways and dark aisles.

James scoops up Toe Beans. The cat mews in protest. "I just don't think this is a good idea."

"We're separated, remember? I can do what I want." You know you're being petty, but you can't help yourself. Your skin is prickling. Withdrawal needling you like a tattoo gun.

* * *

The industrial steel door is thrust open with force, halting just inches from your face. It blocks your view of James across the room from where he left you by the double doors to the kitchen. The door swings back and you once again see the huddle of gold uniforms. The group of them looks over at you.

You find yourself wishing you could hide in the dark dark. Shake *that* lunatic thought from your withdrawal-addled brain.

James walks back over to you.

"I explained the situation. And they do understand the unique circumstances. But this also isn't a good time to let someone new on staff."

"Why not?"

He doesn't answer you.

You can feel the black tendrils squeezing the walls of the mansion. Just the thought of the dense, dark air suffocates you.

"James, I can't go back out there!"

"I never said you had to; there are other Shine Houses. You'll be transferred to one," he assures you, "once arrangements can be made."

Your throat unconstricts slightly. "When?"

"Soon."

Now, it's your chest that's tight. "Did you even ask if I could stay here?"

"No." He looks down.

Good, hope the guilt keeps you up at night.

James leaves you in the storage room with Toe Beans.

You entertain yourself with organizing it by color. Cocktail napkins with bleach. Mop heads with pasta noodles. Windex with mouthwash. Once a uniform walks in, but she takes one look at you, at the shelves, and walks right out again.

When it's *about-fucking*-time for him to clock out, James comes to collect the cat, and you.

You follow him, seething, to a vacant room. Pearl satin and rose gold.

He doesn't enter with you.

"Here, you take this one; I'll find another."

He takes the cat with him.

* * *

Hot bath. The tub is so big you could drown in it. And you have a stomach ache. Your belly sticks up out of the water. Over-stuffed and bloated.

The absence of the drums has left a vacant space inside your skull. Nothing to fill it with but regrets.

You find yourself wishing you could sit by the lake for a while.

* * *

The lights are always on.

Every night is an occasion to celebrate.

The gold uniforms still whisper every time you pass by.

James still won't share a bed with you.

"Nothing will happen," you say, hoping he'll make a liar of you.

But either he doesn't trust you or he doesn't trust himself.

He still won't tell you who the mysterious 'we' is or why the food trucks are really being sent out.

You miss seeing him by the lake. Least in that smudge-smeared reflection he was smiling lovingly at you.

You still can't sleep, even with a night light on.

You haven't been shipped out yet, but it can't be long.

The tendrils tighten.

* * *

It's gotta be the twentieth room you try. It looks like the interior designer of this one was the love child of Liberace and Marie Antoinette. Everything is patterned—scalloped shells and curlicues—from the daybed to the vanity to the upholstered footstools. Mirrors, mirrors everywhere. There's a fucking crystal chandelier over the four-poster.

James is drowning in an oceanic, powder blue, ruffled duvet with matching bed skirt and shams (before James, you had no idea what shams even were). He's crying.

This room would be enough to make anyone overwhelmed.

"What's the matter, muffin top?"

He looks up. Hastily wipes his eyes. "What are you doing here?" he asks in that voice he uses when he's trying to hide that he's upset.

Because I'm trying to save my ass. "Because I'm not ready to give up on us."

"Not now, please." James covers his face with a large ruffle. The cat-sized lump of ginger fur in his lap twitches its tail.

You enter the gaudy room. Close the door behind you. Not even a squeak of a hinge. This place would be lethal in the dark dark.

You approach the bed and sit down beside him—sink down. This duvet is thicker than all the blankets you've ever owned, combined, no exaggeration.

"Why are you crying?"

"Because . . . I'm trying to save humanity," he says into the frill. "You wouldn't understand."

"Try me."

"I—" James hesitates. You can tell he wants to spill. "—can't."

"You can." You pull the ruffle away from his face. "Tell me, muffin top."

"I can't." His voice shifts from despair to resolve. "And I don't have a fucking muffin top any more."

If you can't get him to let you in you'll be sent to some other house. And some other house doesn't have a history with you. Some other house almost certainly wouldn't think twice about sending you back into the black if you fucked up. And let's be real . . .

"So what, you're saving humanity by dancing around in a gold Speedo?"

"Excuse me?" he asks slowly.

"You say you're trying to save humanity, but you're certainly comfortable doing it. Grinding up on these daddies while you eat their finger sandwiches and who knows what else. Looks to me like all you're trying to save is your own ass."

Before, sometimes the only way you'd get James to open up was to get him mad at you. Really mad at you.

"I *knew* you wouldn't understand."

"Oh, I understand. That you've always thought you were superior to me. You think I'm too unintelligent to understand what's going on, or you don't trust me. Which is it?"

"I never said you were unintelligent. You're *always* reading into things."

"So, you won't tell me because you don't trust me anymore." You stand up and turn your back to him. Dramatic, sure. Effective? Hopefully.

"I won't tell you because I don't know you anymore."

Well, that backfired.

"You know me. We're married."

"Separated."

"Does it matter?!" you turn and yell down at him.

"Yes!" He's suddenly standing, too.

Toe Beans hisses under the bed.

"It was less than a year ago," you argue. "We still have a shared bank account, for fuck's sake."

"Bank accounts aren't relevant anymore! A lot can change in a year!"

If he only knew how true that was.

You go all in. "I still love you. That hasn't changed for me."

That's it. No more cards.

"I still love you, too." If James says it, he means it; that sincerity again. "You're here, aren't you? But this is bigger than that."

"There's *nothing* bigger than that."

And he collapses. Clings to you. Like you're an airplane wing in the ocean and he's just crash-landed.

* * *

You ask; he answers.

You want to ask it all before he changes his mind. But the information flows as freely from him as photons from a cracked flux box.

He tells you how the light rich are building a city above the ionosphere.

Project AirGlow.

All the power, the flux, the electrical grid, the retrofit gyms— it's all being siphoned off to build it.

And to build it, people are dying. Graveyards of people.

The trucks are sent out to gather a larger labor force. The canned goods are just so that labor force doesn't starve first.

"So, a few greed-driven asswipes are stealing all the energy so that they can build a city above the dark dark for themselves with forced labor from Mrs. Smith down the street?" you summarize. "That checks."

"It gets worse. They're planning to move their food resources to AirGlow."

"What about everyone else?" As you ask it, you already know the answer. "They're gonna let everyone starve?"

"Everyone who can't buy their way up there."

"They're taking staff though?" Forgot to filter. *Fuck.* Hopefully, it comes off as concern for James and his colleagues and not pure, shameless, self-preservation.

"Oh, you don't have to worry about that."

You're surprised to see his bloodshot eyes smiling.

* * *

Pillow talk reveals everything.

There is a plan. To sabotage Project AirGlow. Make the light rich live in the dark like everyone else. The 'we' is a large portion of the staff who are in on it.

"If we sabotage AirGlow, then they'll just build another one. We need to cripple their infrastructure." James pauses for effect. "The power grids."

"So instead of rich fucks having power, no one will?"

"Humanity will live in light when they learn to work together."

Jesus fucking— James always was an idealist. Probably why he stayed with you longer than he should have.

"It sucks for the people stuck out there, believe me, I *know*."

You sense the people outside the walls of the Shine House displacing the air like worms displacing the dirt in the black black beneath your feet. "But *some* of us have made it. And wouldn't it be better for at least a small portion of humanity to survive rather than risk *no one* surviving?"

"We're way past philosophy" James retorts. "But, for the record, the consensus was 'no.'"

"So you want me to die in the dark dark. You might as well bury me alive."

"You know," he says gently, "this is exactly why we didn't work. You have a bad habit of thinking of everyone else last."

"I'm sorry if I don't have that kind of faith in humanity. But you don't know what it's like out there," you start to argue, but then trail off . . . How do you convey to him hopelessness as heavy as the darkness? Bleakness black as a cave. That people are either desperate to survive or resigned. Just waiting to die. All you manage is, "No one has a purpose anymore. Except maybe the fucking drummers."

"Drummers?"

"Some nut jobs back home are drumming out the seconds. To keep track of time."

"Sounds like a headache."

"My point exactly! People have lost it out there, James. A crazy lady tried to feed me to her cats!"

"OK, we're gonna circle back to that later," he says with genuine alarm. "But listen—" *Shit.* You know that look. The *I-know-these-eggs-are-10x-more-expensive-than-the-regular-eggs-but-they're-the-morally-right-eggs-to-buy* look. "I get that it's terrifying, but it's the right thing to do." Yup, *that* look. "We can give the power, *literally*, back to the people. And whatever happens," he puts his hand on your shoulder, "we're in it together this time."

He leans in. His eyes close for the kiss.

You can hear the distant drumbeat beckoning you from across the black black abyss—*louder, faster*. Then you realize it's only your own heart beating on your ribs.

You want to shake him, to scream at him, but you keep your voice soft as candle light. "So, when is this happening? How is this happening?"

"When it happens, you'll know. Better you don't know the how."

"Because you don't trust me." *Proof!*

"Because I'm protecting you."

* * *

You notice it now. How the gold uniforms exchange whispers when they pass by each other with their polished platters of cocktails and finger sandwiches. If you close your eyes, you can sense it; whatever it is they're planning, it's happening soon.

The spandex of your own uniform shimmers with photons. They glisten off the crystal glasses and jeweled guests and stream up through the skylight—that fluxbeam glow—like a lighthouse illuminating the way to Project AirGlow being built somewhere high above where the stars can still be seen.

* * *

Your shift has ended. You've both peeled the tiny gold uniforms from each other's bodies and are now lying naked on glitter-covered sheets.

You look over at James, skin sparkling, sweat glistening. There's no changing his mind about crippling the power grids. You know your husband. His halo is too bright.

You can see no other way, even with every light switch around you flipped on. So, you tell him, "I want to help." And before he can protest, "We're in it together this time."

* * *

You bathe in sun lamps and dance under prismed chandeliers.

You sip sparkling champagne as rainbows gloss across the surface of bath bubbles.

You see the needle now when you stick it in.

You don't need the drugs to see your surroundings, but you do need them to see that golden hair, shining like the sun that reflected off the water of the lake that day you decided he was your one.

When you pass by the other waitstaff and the moth people brought in for pursuits—pleasurable and perverse—you no longer say your lost one's name. You do not want to know what happened to James when you ratted him out in exchange for a spot on AirGlow.

Instead, you ask a different lost one's name. "Ian?"

That person you were. Before the sun never rose. He's lost forever now.

ACKNOWLEDGMENTS

Thank you to *Nicholas Daniluk* for the original chalk pastel cover art. To *Meghan Witherow-Hunt* for being our encouraging group proofreader. To all our advanced readers, especially and specifically *Bob Proehl* and *Rodney Spivey-Jones* for their generous reviews. And to the *Spring Writes Literary Festival* in Ithaca, NY for providing a community platform to debut this book.